I0730259

Ezra's Head and Other Stories

•

Ezra's Head and Other Stories
a novella and stories

all rights reserved
copyright © 2025, David Kuhnlein
publisher: *tragickal*

cover design by Eunika Sot
edited by *tragickal*

Sean Kilpatrick provided formative edits on much of the original manuscript and Diane Williams edited "The Call to Prayer."

Stories and excerpts have been featured in *OOMPH!*, *Fine Print*, *NOON*, *Bruiser*, *tragickal*, *Hobart*, *Sleepingfish*, and *American Vulgeria*.

Art is revenge masquerading as healing

www.tragickal.com
ISBN 978-1-7387830-2-1

Ezra's Head

and Other Stories

a novella and stories by David Kuhnlein

•

introduction by Brian Evenson

tragickal

TABLE OF CONTENTS

Introduction by Brian Evenson.........................7

Straits of Mackinac....................................11

Dominique...15

The Call to Prayer....................................17

The Rain Made Nudity Impossible.......................21

Fruit in Reverse......................................23

The Disabled..25

Tens and Twenties.....................................29

The Bone Home...31

The Bear Pit..35

Wonderland..37

Ezra's Head...59

IN
TRO
DUCT
ION

THE VAST majority of books have a comfortable relation to the culture in which they exist. They either don't challenge the norms of the culture—often even reinforcing and reifying those norms—or they transgress in ways that quickly feel... predictable. The books that are genuinely transgressive, that disorient you, that get you off balance and keep you off balance in a way that sticks with you and can't be dismissed, are very small in number indeed. But David Kuhnlein's *Ezra's Head* is one of them.

Consisting of nine quite short stories, many just a page or two long, one slightly longer story, and one novella, *Ezra's Head* feels like a series of desperate breaths, followed by a panic attack, followed by a hypoxia-induced hallucination.

The opening short story, "Straits of Mackinac," offers a version of the United States in the midst of collapse. In Kuhnlein's stylized phrasing, "The country had put many a cigarette out on itself." It's a different United States than the one we live in (despite our country's own masochistic cigarette burns), or maybe one just a little farther along the path we seem to be stumbling along. But... it's not that different. There's a hopelessness here, the only proper response to which, the story seems to imply, is violence. Waste, in many of these stories, abounds: the sludge of oil and other pollutants, roadkill, human bodily waste, blood.

Kuhnlein isn't so much interested in pinning down the worlds he creates as in implying a few of the details of these worlds and then letting us fill in the gaps. Occasionally, as we begin to get comfortable, he says something to draw us up short and throw us off-kilter again.

What Kuhnlein is most interested in is language, in the way sentences both convey meaning and obscure it. His style often seems clear and transparent, but the perspective stays close enough to the characters themselves that a lot remains inexplicable. "The baby," says a man in one of these stories, "I think we should eat it." The response a woman gives to this is not what we might expect: "That's funny... I was thinking the same thing." No judgment, no return to the safe ground of "It's wrong to eat babies." But the paragraph that follows is even more destabilizing, since it shifts the parameters of the dilemma: "We started looking forward to the weather's revolutions. We called each other murderer, swirled one another's faces with red paint. My bones quivered between her teeth, softer than tapioca bubbles. We lost all track of time." The first and last sentence seem to have more in common with one another than with the two sentences between them, almost as if something repressed has bubbled up and surged up mid-paragraph, like the bloody head shooting up suddenly in Hegel's Night of the World. Have they eaten the baby? Is the red "paint" blood or just paint? What does it mean for his bones to quiver between her teeth? What's actually happening there? And then there's the oddness of the bones being "softer than tapioca bubbles," something that sounds like the perspective of the person actually feeling the bones between her teeth rather than of the owner of the bones itself. Or is all of this simulated? All speculation and storytelling?

Each of these minimalist nine stories possesses such moments of destabilization and slipperiness, but this comes most fully to fruition in the title novella, "Ezra's Head." The novella is not about someone named Ezra—though it does begin with a quote from Ezra Pound and a character does think of a Pound poem while choking someone. Instead it's about a man named Redd Beyward, living with his grandmother and a pill-popping aunt, who decides to kill himself over his "half-crazed girlfriend"—or, as the story obliquely puts it, "to line his innards with an entire pharmacy in her honor." There are voices that seem to be coming from the walls, and Redd may (or may not) eventually be dead. He may be seeing things, or perhaps these things are really there.

I won't say much more because I don't want to give too much away. At its best, "Ezra's Head" gathers the force of the kind of hallucination that leaves you tingling and unable to distinguish the real from the unreal. Indeed, the accomplishment of the collection as a whole is that it leaves you uncertain not only if the ground beneath your feet is stable, but of whether any ground *anywhere* is. *Ezra's Head* is a deftly textured and beautifully malicious examination of the possibilities of literary destabilization.

– Brian Evenson

STRAITS OF MACKINAC

P AUL WORKED around the clock testing and tinkering with millions of dollars worth of oil cleanup equipment specifically designed for the arctic environment of the Mackinac Straits. Surrounded by a quarter of the world's freshwater, he rebranded the steel in increments, a human squeegee prepared to wipe away the spill. The dog needed cleaning too, hindleg circling its itch. They sat warped by shadow. Organs hung like bats inside them.

Paul's neighbors killed each other over a hazmat suit they didn't know how to strap themselves into. The country had put many a cigarette out on itself. Silver locust trees glistened. Emerald ash coated each branch. If they fell on a hiker, the screams would go unheard. Paul and his friends painted their boats black for night fishing. Gathered by a space heater, they popped Adderall and wrote letters to representatives, an anachronistic frivolity. Bubba suggested bar hopping, even though everything was closed. Sharing moonshine, they felt like their forefathers. Distances were mapped, hard drives scrutinized, shattered glass practiced for, blinds shut.

The buttons on the inside of the Ford Explorer had tiny pictures on them. Paul twiddled a thumb into one, the ceiling of sky deepening. Soon the laminate would peel right off America. There she was, in the crosshairs of his night-vision goggles, dash-cam recorded, seeping down the sidewalk like a ghost. Her cream-colored pantsuit swished. Every point of contact where clothes met skin was where he'd like to cut.

Brandon was leaning against a log stack, smoking, flicking ash over his head. "Go grab some kindling." A pressure squeezed Paul's chest. There was nothing peaceful about the night. This crew was the detritus of better recognized militias. Social media road rage scattered them. Everyone was on someone's list. No digital links existed. No GPS. They were more forest than the forest, now bulging with scientific trail cams, off-road wheelchair accessibility, microbiologists scooping pond scum into a technological diaper. The meeting place was a grounded deer blind. Crumbling fragments formed the roof and wall, assembled and disassembled every meeting.

Paul parked outside the governor's, watching windows light up. The amount of money most people made was public. Paul poisoned himself with this data. The unbearable cries of his newborn, who wouldn't latch, gnawed him. Parts he never knew began to chafe. Stocking ammunition only fixed so much. Paul, Brandon, and Bubba wore balaclavas beneath their goggles. The back of their military fatigues decorated in black letters: "Liberty or Death." Her summer mansion was perched above a golf course. The brick chimney around back afforded all the weight required to scale. A former plumber, Brandon was used to fitting down small spaces in the dark.

The governor and her husband, lit by the television, were covered in sugary crumbs. Paul considered what she might end up doing to get out of the situation they'd put her in, to get back to this particular boredom. It was dark inside. The only distinguishable sound was a battery-operated clock. Brandon ascended the pulley system hoisted around the chimney. Bubba was stationed at the front door. Paul gave the go-ahead via Bluetooth. Brandon slipped through the window and went live. Everything lime green. The ambient light amplified thousands of times created a field of vision. There were no creaks. Just the sound of two out-of-synch snores. The whine of the tube. Nothing as empathetic as a dog. Alarm systems handled. Brandon lifted the sheet with the tip of his knife and revealed their bodies. The governor's silk jammies clung to her. Brandon stepped closer and pressed damp rags over both of their mouths. Their eyes snapped open, then shut. The base stench of the house swerved upon Bubba's entrance. They left food, drink, and reading material for the husband, locked in his own panic room. She burped reflux on the car's plastic seating.

They'd seen enough overseas not to need to rape her. The cameras were in place. Her gag was almost ready. Bubba's wino wife was a beautician. She applied the makeup. The governor awoke, shit-eating grin in place. They explained that there were bombs lining the pipeline. "Remember the Unabomber? Small fry." Bubba ripped out her gag.

As the governor calculatedly prepared a response, Paul shot her in the throat for her effort. The head snapped forward with a flood of skull. "Film that shit till the batteries die..." Paul mumbled into the screams of his friends. They drew on him, frozen, until he walked out of range.

DOMINIQUE

THERE WAS no victim to telephone when Dominique was released. No car corroded by road salt idled outside the gate. He stood alone against the surgery of winter, streetlights foaming into haloed beer.

I watched him hop the chain-link fence across from my house. Sat between us was a median ripped to clay. He had an awkward gait. The arms remained steady. He jogged over while I rolled trash to the curb. We used to wrestle on the same team. They called him "the hammer" because he had to be tucked and taped into his singlet. He could have played jump rope with his own skin.

"Party you had the other night looked fun." I told him to come next time. He said he'd get his daughter a sitter.

The roaches didn't care if he paid rent on time. His neighbors acted afraid of him. "Don't know why, though." He knew people who wrote award-winning plays on the inside and others with every material luxury that offed themselves once free.

I passed an elevator I didn't trust. "...and when the people of Detroit make voting a habit, it'll be a habit they continue to feed," his daughter twisted the radio until the knob clicked. She was the same age we were when we smelled like a shared gym locker. The flavor we wanted to squeeze out of life had changed. She grabbed a ripped trash bag full of clothes, holes growing from where she clutched the plastic. I heard him yell down the hall. His knuckles bulged like a tractor tire. Waiting for the taillights of the girl's mom to round the corner, he tossed me a thick pair of gloves. "Jeans are best for this kind of thing."

Snow calved off the passenger door when I slammed it. He backed up the truck. I lowered the tailgate. On three we lifted the carcass by its legs into the bed. The deer looked alive, caffeinated, black eyes bulging like marbles. The next two were less intact.

The farmer called himself a renegade monk. We caught him in our high beams, sledgehammering a hole in the pond. "So the cows can take a drink," he said. These carcasses would distract pests from his cabbage. He yanked an axe from cavities remotely resembling a deer, pulled at the ribcage, scraping guts into a bucket.

There was so much I didn't recognize. My thoughts, vicariously gutted, got stuck in a popped socket. We swallowed traces of blood from the leaden air. I flipped wood chips atop what he chopped. Putzing along the bumpy trail, windshield wipers slashing flakes, chucking deer parts into empty spaces in the wall, filling in the sinister tessellation, covering last month's frozen gristle with scraps, we awaited the stink of when everything would thaw.

THE CALL TO PRAYER

"WHAT IS your boy's name?" he said, jarringly.

"Gabriel."

The boy wore one orange kitchen glove.

"Want to see something?" the boy said.

"How do you say?" the woman said. "It fell in the water tank. He saved her. This... rat?"

"Had a couple myself," the man pointed to his apartment, "in the walls. And I saw that they had tons of traps when they cooked me biryani down there," he said, gesturing to the flat below.

A whiff of rot reached them. The space between the homes, just enough to shimmy through, was hardly large enough for a puddle. Rain that fell on Hamtramck smelled like marijuana smoke. Sometimes the man's disgust couldn't be stopped. The skin-and-bones pit-mix was leaking piss as if alive, surrounded by dung heaps. The glassed-in porch did not contain the smell.

"Smart kid. How old is he?"

"Nine."

Gabriel kept the rat in a towel and cupped it to his chest. The man couldn't remember the last time he saw a face so crisp in real life, the rat's face.

"I rescued all kinds of animals when I was a kid. Rabbits, dogs, birds," the woman said.

"Where was that?"

"Poland."

"Rural?"

"What?"

"In a city?"

"Yes, big city, big apartment buildings."

"Which?" he asked, though he couldn't name any cities in Poland.

"Rzeszów," she said. "Near Kraków."

"I've heard of Kraków."

"It's..." She used her hand to demonstrate where they lived in Poland. He didn't know Poland was shaped like a hand. Her nails had dirt under them. He felt naked without someone else's mess. His feminine hands embarrassed him. She pointed to the fatty tissue beneath her thumb.

"Last year he fixed a pigeon and named it Oscar," she said, pointing to Gabriel. "It was a baby he taught to fly. It went," she twisted her hand into the air, "like this. It came back to us. We put it on..."

"The roof," Gabriel assisted with the word.

"Yes, it came when we call: Oscar, Oscar. In the morning, it waited on the steps. It's gone."

The man was wondering about a potential connection

between his attraction to the woman and his inability to remember her name when several men, one wielding a shovel, showed up in the alley.

Three years ago, the woman mentioned in passing how it wasn't safe to walk around after dark. If she wanted to take nighttime walks, he said he'd be more than happy to accompany her. Her habit was to subtly decline him.

Before the man's occiput got crushed, before his wrists cracked against swinging steel, splintered beyond repair, before he was called a faggot while his ribs were kicked in, before the ringing in his ears sounded like trumpets, he hoped the woman would find him and use the rest for compost.

THE RAIN MADE NUDITY IMPOSSIBLE

I WANTED to stay friendly enough to get called on the phone and, from time to time, fucked.

Having feelings only takes a bit of practice. And, for whatever reason, this seemed to be the key to the kind of heart I was looking to parasitize, ever since my boredom had eclipsed everything else. Being home alone was like trying to entertain a cat.

The phone rang. I pressed the vibration against my forehead, long enough to see things. Before the last pulse, I answered: "Have you made up your mind?"

"It gets old talking about the void all the time."

I stirred the spaghetti with one hand and cradled the phone in the other. The sauce thickened her voice.

Meatballs dodged a wooden spoon beneath small bubbles.

"The baby," I said, "I think we should eat it."

"That's funny." There was a long pause before she finished the thought, "I was thinking the same thing."

We started looking forward to the weather's revolutions. We called each other murderer, swirled one another's faces with red paint. My bones quivered between her teeth, softer than tapioca bubbles. We lost all track of time.

Spring sounded against the roof. Rain punctured each poncho, lashing exposure, cold as medication.

We copy and pasted the email associated with a craigslist ad headed: WILL PERFORM MOST SURGICAL PROCEDURES.

His singular status had coddled him. White hair spritzed beneath his military-style cap. He was trained in a war. I didn't ask which. Our emails back and forth consisted mostly of him complaining about a world I wasn't sure was real. He didn't want compensation or validation—he needed a spittoon. I opened my mouth, obligingly.

FRUIT IN REVERSE

THE FIRST girl, the bicyclist, backpedaled through every story she told me, claiming it wasn't hers to tell. We spent many afternoons trying to yank my fingers from her hair. Her flesh wanted out of those spats, they were the first thing I saw of her, and I munched through bitter pears toward them, dreaming. Neither of us showered. We only used soap for sentimental reasons. Sadly, and immediately, I fell in love.

But I was already in love with a girl who chewed her hair to foam. Between bites, she begged for incest. "Let's wear each other's clothes," she insisted. This girl disappeared into the distance but overwhelmed me up close. In this period of my life, beneath the bake of our one fluorescent light that hummed like a tattoo gun, kissing meant more than it should've. After a daylong hiatus in our relationship, it was clear she was in several others. I misread her need to spoil these other connections for love.

Before them, I pined for a girl with a diamond drilled into her lateral incisor. Built like a pickup, her hair cartoonishly bobbed across the strawberries. She loved to ride our communal bike. I thought of her every time something funny-smelling rose from the seat. I brushed my teeth with her image. She was cute in the way that a bumblebee is cute, striking quickly then dying.

We all lived on a farming cult. It was a line of belief better than most horizons. I was sedated from mimicking the sun. Only blankets hung between me and the women. I slept directly on the tile, increasingly injecting my thighs with biologic drugs, while my ribs and shoulders, like fruit in reverse, bruised for a week and then ripened.

THE DISABLED

THE STINK of Lysol and mouth foam peculiar to most mental patients, followed by what might have been kindly referred to as Genghis Khan eyes, sat in my car, unhinging its hair. She'd grown everyone around her into a cyst without circumference. Her moons waned in me. Our collective urge to self-destruct flattered suburban crackheads. All the interstices of pain she came to cultivate stood polluted through a lust not given lightly. Barren from poking at herself too long: "I've been bullied by many endoscopies," she mocked. These disassembled memories spent like antibodies, petite sufferings left uncured.

Her mouth moved strangely, like the injustice of the creature it obeyed. "What do I have to do? Walk around in high heels all day just to get a couple painkillers? Anytime I see these quacks they treat me like I've just crawled out from the dirt, a fucking junkie. And they're still selling love and light like an unendowed alchemist." We passed the house of a sister scared of her punk-like shadow. The mother's house was off limits. We squeezed every last muscle relaxer from her armoire. "Open the glove box," I said, "I geocached a souvenir from my sister's suicide." She flipped it open and the weight of the gun lugged against the plastic with a thunk.

Each trip to the ward was an opportunity to develop her ailments. Phrases wagged around through that Polaroid of a mind, aphorisms from some evil, New Age, bio-hacking rhetoric. She tried to hypnotize herself into action, to collect the raining stalactites of painkillers, plunk them into the palms of those in need. "There's a Robin Hood for every sick and lifeless schmuck. For those who can't do laundry without Tylenol 4, or walk the dog without a Soma."

Those drugs had a cult of their own side effects. But a couple addicts later and all the people with intractable pain swallowed the sharp end of the stick, unyielding the chronic and persistent edge, bone against sharpened bone. The sky filled out scripts and held them over our heads. Stinky babies, lawless, no muscular definition, rolls of fat abounding—this was what gravity had done to everyone. Nothing existed outside of its cave. "If you need to warm up, I just peed myself," she said. I debased her fundamentalist hysteria with an electric blanket.

Watching Jack Kevorkian on Netflix, the cutie popped her last painkiller, "I don't know how much longer I can do this, begging for weak codeine, its anaphoric drone." She started sleep-talking about messy stints in jail. There were people unworthy of love. There were almost no people worthy of love. Opioids fixed that. To live without a clock on the wall, in the heart of your personal Hollywood, pardoned by quacks.

I decided to help her. White caps and orange bottles scattered across the lawn. I saw her springing on rooftops, slinging a Santa sack filled to the brim with Dilaudid. Such a menace, balancing the DEA's reticule. I chanted a mantra about becoming wood, relearned facial expressions in the mirror, better than a lie detector. Shell casings splashed the hospital floor. I scrubbed my prints from the gun for an hour. I returned to her, hands and knees, trembling in her blue, fluorescent glow. My dreamy death witch, hari-kari Krishna.

TENS AND TWENTIES

NOTHING IN the world, no feeling I got from women, love, or yearning, compared with opening the woodstove door, waiting for the cloud of ash to settle, and admiring the stack of tens and twenties I received at the end of each month.

The woodstove awkwardly took up most of my bedroom, which could not truly be called a bedroom—really, it was a hallway I slept in. I could reach my arms out and touch the wall on one side and the window to the lean-to on the other. A sheet tacked between my hallway and the living room was my only door. The herbalist dragging a hose behind her, wanting to wet her seedlings, or even a tiny draft, exposed me to the commons. People came and went as they pleased, often forgetting to step over my sleeping body.

I tucked my money among the wood ash, because not even elbow deep in chicken shit did I feel dirty, let alone in a calcium-carbon compound, and I figured that the stove would be the last place anyone would look. I was right. Séraphine, the Mexican migrant who mailed his cash back to his wife and daughter, beat the shit out of his son when I caught the boy rifling through my stuff. That little thief unholstered every item from my wallet, bleaching them in the windowsill's light. When I heard the boy's yelps through the thin walls of their trailer, I wanted to feel bad, but I didn't.

Before I left to live on the farm, my roommate Lee gave me a beautiful set of chopsticks. Two glass mallard ducks were included in the intricate box, upon which the chopsticks would lay when not in use. Lee was shy and stared at my rug when I thanked him.

I didn't tell him that I'd watched him purchase this box the week before, after we attended a matinee of Miyazaki's recent release. As Lee lay his items on the conveyer belt at Hua Xing, including the ornate box, I fingered a rolled-up twenty in my hip pocket, thickened by its hamburger folds. I have my suspicions as to why I didn't offer to pay, as he'd bought our movie tickets, but, like the tens and twenties, I'll keep them to myself.

THE
BONE
HOME

THE MAN feels fingered into a wet knot by his own municipal culture. The Beagle and the Labrador follow a carrot. Their leash, disappeared inside his jacket, is cutting him. Sleeves down over chapped skin, he shucks a sweater from each dog's wagging ass. They wobble themselves stood. Only crumbs for treats remain. Fingers pressed into the pain in his temple, fishing for relief, he can't decide how to divide the dregs between them. It is the kind of suburb often stunned silent by digestible lives. A neon witch horizon traverses the garage on an infinite loop.

The dogs yip Pig Latin all night. The man washes, lights off, avoiding eye contact with the mirror. In bed, he picks his nose and wipes the waxy ball against the scar tissue of others. Wind rips leaves from the branches, as if loosening their way through layers of rabbit cadaver, crackling sticky beneath fur. Yellow light, crowded on his face, breathes in and out. He reaches up, into the darkness, and taps the machine awake, moves through YouTube clips and webpages that exist only for themselves. Then the gelatin of sleep.

Lack of breakfast stabs his stomach more than pills. Halfway to starvation, the dogs gnaw flea-ridden hides. They no longer have enough energy to run in their dreams. Rubber boots laced, whispering snouts shoved indoors, he stomps the bent step, cutting edge shot into soil, and rediscovers a cheesecloth after three shovelfuls of earth. Every piece of the sack is accounted for, seasons later, seams split on all sides, brown and bloated.

The Bone Home
337 Madrugada Dr
Hell, MI 48169

He awaits a payment, refreshing the page. His wrists ache. His teeth feel rotted to the gum. Soon he'll be forced to drink synovial fluid. Flies pick open a scab on the Labrador's unflinching head. Feelers pinch vanquishing skin. Soon there won't be an inch of dog visible. A cracked latticework has bloomed fungal in the cobwebs of its bowl. The man limps back outside, collar in one hand, shotgun in the other, the black mass dragged and whining. The flies resettle on their meal at the noise. The man adds a bit of burying room to the hole.

Palms together above the heat of the monitor, he mumbles an exclamation when a payment arrives. Included is a short message from the dealer: *Hard to keep domestic cat bones in stock. We appreciate doing business.* Even as money returns to the household and the pantry shelf begins to sag from the weight of white rice and biscuits, the Beagle ignores him, missing its friends. An afternoon walk is their only shared experience. The man strokes his computer, whispering, "Kitty cat, kitty cat, where have you gone." The Beagle eats because it enjoys the sensation of its long tongue following into its stomach. Axial skeleton grinding through malnutrition, it starts sneaking into the cabinet when the man sleeps. After a month, they're both scratching their fleas again. The Beagle muzzles open National Geographic magazines, making sure that pages filled with starfish, short-tailed crickets, rat snakes, and other self-cannibalizing creatures catch the morning light.

The man is busy trying to figure out what roadkill is most lucrative, and how many domestic dog bones are stocked but not sold. He owns one more shotgun shell. But he gets another idea. Working through the night, sterilizing equipment, he fashions a contraption with an ax, loads of string, and a large weight. Lidocaine particles tickle the air, but it's not enough. Biting a rolled-up tee-shirt, the man screams, shaking the foundation of the house. The first drop of the blade runs halfway guillotined. The inside of the man's wrist looks like marmalade. The Beagle crosses its paws, head atop them, exhaling deeply.

THE
BEAR
PIT

They have tied me to a stake; I cannot fly,
But, bear-like, I must fight the course.
   – *Macbeth*

SHE TREMBLES with the snowmelt, as if meaning to keep cold. I hold my bladder, watching. A chime is answered, voluntary pathogen pressed in the inner ear. We flag an app taxi. Her taps pillow ash on Astroturf. We've tried being clean. It's entertaining. Rubber-banded grocery bag snapped overhead, plump lips lit by sparkling Retina Display, she intones: "I'm sick of everyone claiming they're a survivor. You didn't survive shit." Her thumb drills the screen. "Just being a victim's never enough." I encourage some thoughts being saved from the feed.

Pop-up arena approaching, animals taped together in a scream. Large metal rings gouge the beast's limbs, industrial stigmata carved in. Runes etched on the muzzle fill blackly, vaginal upper gums pinned back. Directing the head of the moon bear, a crew of tiny men saw it some nubs. Canine teeth chiseled down. A canal in the cheek bone shows optic nerves. Eyes removed from sockets sutured shut. Hamstrung by a goose quill saber, baritone vibrations still felt underground. The splotches on its chest look pissed there.

We'd let a sneeze release what ailed us, if it wasn't our finest possession. Sticking out our necks for secret events, ballooning past the scientific mediocrity of life, is worth seeing a bear cling to a ridge pole. Cigarette smoke flits between the tectonic plates in my head. Nineties rave for a brain, I reduce myself to strobe lights. A cripple on a tricycle circles the crowd, playing music from a Bluetooth speaker. Her hips sway on mine. I'm in it for the notch I'll make in her web. Spectator deaths do occur. Many of us are strapped. The audience is on the same plane as the spectacle, a well-seasoned subspecies. Lots of top dogs bobbing at the trough. The bear's muscles exhaust. The blood vessels of its eyes bloat. They unveil dog cages. Pit-mixes and mastiffs sharpen their teeth against the floor.

At first, I did not love her. The drive to stun and steal women from themselves frightens me. But I hadn't met someone to be cruel with. My remains went unmatched, save for her. "Don't grieve," she assuages me through barbeque smoke. Sometimes I dilate her nostrils with my tongue to see if she's frowning beneath all that scarred and overlaid skin. The bear continues dying on the pole, really committing to the Kegels of each throe. It's chained to wood, secured by a ring in the nose. A harmony has formed between beast and crowd. Strands and fibers merge in matted fur. I feel her smile through the blinding sting. Latched as one, we tease our arms forth for one last bite, because this is religion.

WONDERLAND

They all answered to his name, those ghosts he felt each morning slipping into his clothes as he dressed.

– John Edgar Wideman, *Hurry Home*

Damita

MIMI CALLED during Scorpio season, which is every season here, her voice coy behind the static of my cordless. I listened as she detailed the crime scene that my brother had chalked himself into. His right hand, she said, had clutched the family's Phillips head, which he'd plunged into his intercostal, the cartilage between his ribs, and was still clawing the black and yellow handle when she returned with groceries. If there were convulsions, involuntary muscle spasms, or anything denoting a dying and not a dead man, they had since ceased. My brother had turned himself into a stiff.

"I kept looking for a spot to put the bags," Mimi said. "Couldn't find the counter. Lost track of the floor."

She said it felt like the whole house had receded to a single hair follicle. Brown puddles climbed her high heels, slushing outward from her boy's heart. It was in that mud that she awaited the footprints of his ghost. His split lips looked like wax pressed into a tongue. I didn't question any of this, though I've no clue what she meant. I didn't yet know what it was like to lose a child.

Over the years, my brother's chest had grown concave, shoulders hunched forward until they nearly touched, neck bent elliptically—as if he could roll past middle age and into death, as if he could bypass the caretaking that his schizophrenia already, and embarrassingly, required from Mimi. Each cornea had grown milky with bloodshot. Whether he was trying to ignore or impress the voices, it was clear that neither worked. I had Mimi move in with us. We were, after all, three generations of Harrises from a different dad.

D'Wayne, my four-year-old, had never minded the rats. "That boy'll be lucky to wake with both limbs," Mimi insisted when she wasn't weeping. My dead brother had, supposedly, once snacked on a tortured rat, venerating some cat-like God. Mimi carried and set traps everywhere because of her poorly handled guilt. They snapped my shoelaces in half. I needed some breathing room. Punching holes in the drywall of our one-bedroom prevented the feeling of containment from becoming crushing. Though I spackled and sanded the holes before Mimi got back from her shift at the Wonderland Mall. On weekends, I let Mimi babysit the kid and hung out in the restroom of The Last Call, a biker bar, stretching up my bleeding gums between the graffiti on the mirror. Life then felt like leaning out the window of a dream.

Mimi reset the traps I'd tripped, depositing them in concentric circles. "It's an object's unintended use which makes it worthy of study, an element of beauty," she said, and bought a display case for the uncleaned tool that had whispered the last voice my brother ever heard. She had totally lost it.

Telephone wires boxed our house in. Locked pole-barns surrounded and towered over us, almost as dwarfed as my runt standing next to his friends. The pole-barns were probably empty, but nevertheless cut off to the public, only accessible via city officials, with who-knows-what stored away. There was so much information available now that I was utterly reluctant to learn a damn thing.

Striped lounge chairs took on a reptilian bake. December sandwiched us in its weird weather. The breeze flicked D'Wayne's windbreaker. The zipper hit his teeth, like a shrill call to his future. I showed D'Wayne how water crystalized into slush as it fell, shadowed by our hundred-year oak. The way our weathervane strived to represent the birds that defecated beneath it. And how sidewalk cracks looked like an M.C. Escher painting of the scales of an alligator in a post-coital slump.

Although D'Wayne visited these images that I painted in his mind over cereal, he didn't yet have the wherewithal to transcend their destitution... or to communicate displeasure. D'Wayne was a typical little boy, energetic, full of life. He liked to play with unpainted blocks in the dry spaces between the sod, and I pretended to watch him in front of the neighbors, keep up appearances. This life spent in a tracksuit was a mere stopgap for his forthcoming oasis, a pinpoint on the mirage we would together so grossly render.

Less than a year ago, we were financially delivered by a storm that Mayor Kingston Burns cussed up, audible even over the washing machine as I slid off, shivering across the asbestos.

"How many of the Chambers Brothers I gotta nab to keep this city spayed?" He looked brained by his own weight. In his hands he squeezed a prepared bass, flayed for two.

"Takes a long time for these trees to grow from acorns, even longer in this shithole." He bit off a pleasurable chuckle. The bass leaked through the newspaper, stinking up the kitchen. A buzzing fridge stood fat between us. "But when they're planted," he took a handful of dirt from his jean pocket and sprinkled it on the kitchen floor, "they last longer. My nephew tells me you and Mimi are going through it."

"No different than the rest," I said.

He untucked the fish from the waxy paper, spooned tangy sauce on top. "Have a favor to ask, Damita. I get the feeling you're built of tougher stuff..."

At first, I think he trusted me, but in the end was frightened. After I stapled D'Wayne's eyes shut, the muscles around them somehow stayed slack. Trying to keep accusatory glances to a minimum, after my meeting with the mayor, I never laid a hand on the child. Burns allowed a certain amount of creativity on my end. I knew the way I'd let the boy go, warming my filet knife against his masseters, pinkish mandible beneath. "Let a pair of eyes be born for every crime." My carving design made it look like he fell asleep chewing a mouthful of blueberries. Any place D'Wayne went was thickened by his residue.

Three foot nothing. Fifty pounds and wrapped in plastic. His bagged head overripe to the touch. Mom's green lasagna warmed in the oven, forcing air from three cinched bags, flu-like stench pervading, molecularly mingling with the boy's remains. His aura drum rolled above the flesh. There was no more etiquette to ask of him. The seashell racket his death left grew louder at night, which was a common occurrence, even as the stars winced back from the sky.

The Wonderland Mall looked peaceful through my monocular. I slid back the eyepiece. Necks swiveling between items clicked into focus. I scribbled notes like shorthand lightning, faster than the woodpecker sneering down its beak at me. Michigan's bird populace started declining concurrently with my birth. Perhaps a vantage point that high inspired suicide.

Another barren December. "Gonna have a white Christmas, mommy?" What a little sucker. Pestered by a child whose ashy skin could make a light dusting of itself, answering its own question—humans never have any choice but to carry the droppings we are forced to sculpt.

A flock of shoppers poked at Sunday prices. Entryways glowed. Their neon outline jarred me, doppelgangers resurrected through decade-old displays. I leaned the driver's seat back, unclamped the handbrake, and rolled over the dead hill in neutral.

I posed through Target surveillance with slews of others, hair blending with mandated styles, clothes a reasonable color. VHS tapes lured me away, but then I pretended to scold D'Wayne as if he lived. Feigning an outburst with screen value, shouting my ruined name, I halted: "D'Wayne? Sweetheart?" I pored over the racks where kids like to hide so they'd remember my twisted-up face, smiling dumbly at people who'd see me on highlight reels on Channel Four every day for the next month. Finally someone said, "Lose something, miss?"

"I'm looking for my son," I panted. "He's three feet tall and wearing a blue coat."

We searched at a pace, but the employee wouldn't contact someone with more authority. I needed it to be their idea. Not to panic too forcedly. D'Wayne had been upset because I hadn't let him buy the tape he wanted, that was my story. I became frantic as we searched. Security finally decided to call the Livonia Police Department. Then a wider net was cast, including the mall basement, which happened to smell lovely. Nothing was found to indicate D'Wayne's personage at this location. Nothing but the stillness that a job well done provided. Nothing but popcorn shells and Cinnabon crumbs. My hysteria did not appear to be laughter.

The announcement issued by security turned into the longest and largest search for a kid the state had ever seen, and a perfect diversion from Kingston Burns, soon to be Detroit's former mayor. Many of Burns's cadre would soon be arrested, tailed by police, and harassed by the FBI into obscurity, while Burns himself magically evades arrest and steers clear of prison.

Eventually, they interviewed me and Mimi. Others remained behind to start the tedious process of watching footage. They hoped that one of the cameras would show which direction D'Wayne had wandered off in, whether he left the mall with anyone. The microscope they shoved down the front of my jeans remained there for the rest of my life. I slunk under its lens, shrinking one way, swelling another, wishing they'd known. "How alive must the hunted item be?" I thought.

I saw the lion's mane turn red in my redundant Belle Isle Zoo dream, retracting the crisp bone of my arm, sandwiched between the bars of his cage. "He was with me in the mall," I told my therapist, referring to my son they'd never find. I wouldn't be surprised if she was undercover. Video evidence was always an attempt to clarify a life that meant nothing—digital pixels, the phantom of an image. D'Wayne glitched in my periphery. I had a bag with his head in it.

Palmer Park was unobserved. I dragged the bag through a porous batter of snow behind me. My shoes were covered in the dust from our unfinished basement.

I had been told to leave him in the bin by the basketball court. Even my tracks were erased. Other than the shells of cars too old to still be aboveground—their hoods propped open mid-technique—there was no sign of humanity. The vegetation appeared to be left over from another time, all the wrong colors. In the detritus of a construction crew's lunch, a black and white tomato floated in a puddle of sewage and sod. The tomato skin was translucent, recognizable only by shape and context, littered beside other recognizable fast food. A three-legged stray hobbled around the corner and then sniffed the fruit, mechanically shuddering. Two gulping motions and the tomato vanished. We locked eyes. It seemed satisfied, as if it had swallowed a ghost.

D'Wayne

MOST NIGHTS I get terrible sleep. No one tucks me in, and the only story I'm told comes from Pierre, but his voice is muffled by the dirt between us. Because of the sound the water makes plinking against the soil up above, my favorite time of year is when it rains.

I'm only trying to have a one-way conversation, though dictation is a better way to put it, since it's been hard to find a pen, and even harder to find someone willing to inscribe for me in your world what it is I'm dictating from mine, but I have a very dear, sweet, trustworthy, lovely (the list is endless...) friend named Pierre who's agreed to help me so long as I sit still for him once a day, when the sun reaches its peak and the ground warms enough for our joints to wiggle.

Because of his increasingly mottled complexion and the dilating hole in his neck, his coffin seems to be snacking on him while he sleeps. Pierre has the airs of a dead aristocrat, which is contrasted only with the mayoral brand burnt onto his chest, exposed beneath his torn button-up, suggesting that he was to be a retainer sacrifice. He coughs loogies into a Dixie cup, filling one up every ten minutes or so to paint me with his sinuses. His eye is so precise.

"Can I see it?" I ask.

"Tonight," he says. "When it's ready."

Every night before we slip back under our tarpaulins, glad to have not been cremated, he whines: "There," reaching up past black pine triangles of treetop, past the wisps of cloud, tapping with his filthy French fingernail against the black bubble that pumps us in all directions at once.

"See it?" he insists, excited enough for me to know he's not joking. I lie that I do. Ma taught me to be polite. We dread the discomforting thought that God might appreciate us.

Although this document does indeed exist, I understand that the curve of every letter, no less than the arms of my consciousness, or whatever you want to call it, might at first behave quite gaseous in your mind. I hope to branch these arms further, however, as you allow them to ossify within you. I simply want to share, not prove, these miniature details—it's all molehills here—not only to get them off my fifty-pound chest, but so that the ghost I continue to operate as will be able to breathe more clearly. My only regret—because I think you'll see that I love my mother dearly—is not growing old enough to smoke.

"Smoke while you're alive, breathe easier when you're dead." This is Pierre's first aphorism. "Countless shit is of import to the living," he says. It takes the greater part of a day to hear him talk. But what did I have planned? What did I look forward to aside from the stench of my fellow ghost? A stench I'm still not used to.

It's not every day that a four-year-old gathers this much attention. From how it all shook out—I loved watching Ma and Mimi take turns spanking our Welcome mat with the broom, dust clouds settling over the lilacs, but I loved the VCR more—between who I was before Burns realized it was too late for many of his people but not too late for him and who I am now, was now, will be now, forever and ever, there were only so many options. Legality is simply no match for strong desire.

A vehicle's items are engineered purposely too large to be swallowed by the likes of me: large plate window, seat leather, buckles, handles, headrest, but still I licked them down to their core. The stench of my decomposition integrates with insects, slurping gelatinous absorption. I am crinkling inside my oxygen, bacteria in its final war. In my case, I was the intersection of thousands of planar lines webbed planetary. I carve my life into my palm to recall. Rows of teeth crackle in the breeze, death's visage pried apart, watered with sepia poisons. Time to live burnt within a headline. Being outside of time crams you with dictionaries of knowhow. That's why I talk like this.

Years ago, I met Pierre unceremoniously. He was bent at the waist searching for his reflection in the pond, which he claimed to miss. "But at least the fish can see me," he said, mimicking how they bobbed in the water. We are kept astray from our image, though looking down I'm still graced by my Filas and royal blue sweatsuit I was buried in. Sometimes, Pierre wades into the water, searching for dead ones dumb enough to take his bait, he says. I am not confident enough to insult our kin so allegorically. There was nothing in that moment, and to be honest ever since, that I wanted more than to not be speaking with a dead man, to not be who and where I was, and instead be playing with my firetruck between burnt splotches of lawn, mommy calling me in for dinner...

When I was growing up, mom had called me suckfish. I never let the inside of a bottle stay wet. I drank like I ate, till it hurt. In profile, thousands of bead-shaped stomach aches lay between the distance and my eyes. I continue to see the world through four years of tears.

"They say you don't remember before you're three or four," Pierre sighs. The pentagonal lump near his occiput is organized like a filing cabinet. I would always think, but never say, "What a waste!" Sometimes a basketball net is the only cloud in the sky. Airplanes drone their lectures at each other in unheard languages, like mine.

Ma taught me to pick through any emotion with a stick. I salute my sadness because he is a frequent guest. We know much more than one another's name. I remember finding a man in the Fisher Building having a fit in the restroom, chipping a front tooth against the urinal. Somehow he didn't bruise anything. That was when I realized that the living body paints its territories differently. Would I have to thrash around like that in public to have swaths of pretty girls lean over my bed? But still, none of them would compare to Ma.

Sizable worms push free of Pierre's collar. He tears a fat one from its nipple, vessels teething colorfully, and secures it to a fishing hook. "Watch carefully." He casts a line to the center of the pond. Fish dart away. Bodies of fish tap the shore, strewn on his line. "They can't decide between heaven and earth when they're in the water." Pierre clutches the line like a balloon. "If we eat a bunch of them, gravity won't matter." An oval of scum blinks from the pond. This is where we live now, in a secret cemetery behind the Manoogian Mansion.

I've been dead longer than I was ever alive. Movies look too clean now. I miss my mom's perm. Her Medusa weave spoke to me. Mayor Kingston Burns used to wake me up and parade me around the night, trees cremating constellations, bulbs of light evaporating an asymmetric grid cracked by branches, but I think at this point he's forgotten all about me. It has been so long since he dug an apple peeler into my neck, smearing the origin of half a dozen curse words beneath the moonless sky. His pit-mixes took apple-sized bites out of my legs for fun. I still have cartoon teeth marks where flesh didn't grow back. The last time I saw him was the Halloween bash of 1995. Shuffling my feet in the dungeon below, entertaining his company, I heard his voice boom, "Pick up your goddamn feet, boy!" I felt special, as Burns's diction was the stuff of legend. Now I die every night looking at a portrait of myself, painted by Pierre, which is most likely how kings would choose to go if prompted. But who deserves such a repetitive fate, to live and die with the sun?

The mayor's mansion has more lawn workers than residents. The boys are always sweating, bustling over ornamental grass, sprinkling water on the hedges with long fingernails, clicking sprinklers on and off, testing the turgidity of large blue tubes that filter through many layers of lawn. Each flowering shrub and invasive herb is watered to the milliliter. Burns was a stickler regarding beautification. This private cemetery within his compound is no exception. It's a nice place to rest.

"Been a long time since I had someone to paint," Pierre says. I nod, lips pursed, not sure if a response would break the pose. "The last boy always looked constipated, face squinched up with veins I mistook for worms and vice versa. One day he bent over and when I asked him what's wrong... you wanna know what he said?"

I nod.

"Keep your head still! I'm working on your neck."

"That's what he said?" I ask.

"No. You, D'Wayne, keep your head still. The boy, the *other* boy, he said, 'I'm thinking' and then he burst into a thousand worms! I aimed my light but they had slipped into the ground with such speed that I questioned whether or not it happened at all." Pierre drags another worm out from behind his collar. "I used to wonder if these were pieces of him." The worm curls around his finger, cartoonishly sticking out of his grip. "But it's not worth the energy. Besides, how to test a thing like that. I'm an artist. It's him when I need them to be, not when I don't."

Between his dead fish, paint, and boys, I figure I am somewhere in the middle of his triangle of love. Through the top of its head, Pierre gives the worm a metal spine, forcing the hook through its writhing body.

"Art has nothing to do with life," he continues. "It does, however, have everything to do with death." I don't ask. Pierre is working himself into a frenzy. My perspiration includes an echo of the skin it has emerged from. Gravity hurts Pierre's heavier body. He drags pieces of his corpse behind him. I wonder how much longer the ball and socket of his shoulder will be able to wield a brush. "Nothing's ever how it's portrayed. People want representation," he says. He's on one of his diatribes. "It's all smoke and mirrors! Who would want to be distilled to an infinitely replicable beam of light, dictated by zeros and ones? Insanity!"

"I liked when *Family Matters* was on," I tell him.

"Well, you're just a kid, what do you know? Your job is to shut up and be beautiful." Pierre knows that the mind keeps faltering behind consciousness, bombarded with acronyms, equations, systems, and truth. Despite our temporary escape from the worm's digestive slit, I long to nap.

Pierre says we should count our thoughts like calories. Mom often mentioned how I got under her skin worse than the tune of her daily alarm clock. I refuse to haunt my mother in the flesh, hoping that the needles I assume she still talks to at the very least give her something resembling numbness, a momentary reprieve.

"Art is pieces of a puzzle that can make you feel who you are, against your better judgment, and those who produce it with any modicum of skill must have their throats professionally cut. They spoil upon celebration." The only sound, aside from our charred voices, and Pierre's innards filtered through his hip bones, is the frantic dictation of the leaves, like antibodies squirted, uselessly, into this putrid flesh.

Kingston

"I GREW up, uh, pretty close to this river." Mayor Kingston Burns casually gestures to the water then pinches his thick black glasses. Behind him, squirrels ride their tails like jet skis. "When I first came to Detroit in the early twenties, uh, 1923 as a matter of fact, I lived at Saint Aubin and Antietam, three blocks south of Joe Muers."

Having spent no effort on timbre, I plan to edit out my voice in post. It's an untrained mess that doesn't match the rest, though looking at me naked you might say my head doesn't quite fit either, as if it developed of its own accord. I blot out everything in my frame except for the gargantuan banana leaves framing the mayor's salt and pepper beard. Medium shot: his shoulders and neck up, gravelly voice, enough spittle to fill a Dixie cup. My sweater itches me behind the camera, but I don't scratch.

"People tend to gather according to race or ethnicity..." I zoom in on Burns's neck, observing his respiratory rate and carotid artery. The students are what ruined med school for me. I prefer the anatomy of light on screen. When I dropped out to study film, I lied to everyone that I was following my passion. Nobodies made an ice cream cone out of me whether or not I cared (I didn't). Those socially conditioned walls have long since melted.

You might say I've become a bit obsessive about a theory of mine about a child who disappeared the same year Kingston Burns stepped down. It's been two years, two months, and twelve days since the boy's disappearance. Let's give the tabloid of that some heft.

Without the boundary of a lecture hall, I've been free to observe the Manoogian Mansion like it pays the rent (it doesn't). My in finally came last Saturday. A film friend who works for the Detroit Archive Project got the flu. Burns's staff float through here, which I know from stolen blueprints is only one of three sunrooms. His assistant thinks I'm writing him a cinematic love letter.

"I'm Kingston Burns, goddamit!" the man booms, broadcasted. I had tuned him out, not exactly sure what upset him. He leaves the vicinity to relieve himself. I pop out back for a smoke, clutching the luxurious ashtray of a staff member. I suck one down, then take my time with a second. First smoke is for the fix, the next is to think...

All things transform like images in my lens. Even film stills are hard to hold. Grasping by their edges, trying not to ruin the delicate emulsion of my Focal Point Pentacam, it's like trying to erase your childhood by chewing on an old pencil. To the human eye, one image is followed by another until the credits roll. There's no end to this. Montage is our natural state. A man who truly knows how to live wanders this land without ever encountering a hollow point or shank. In him, his wife finds no opening for her fish blade, his children find no wrists to insert their razors. Death has no place in him. But it wasn't death I wanted for the mayor. Sure, I'd like an admission of guilt, some justice for the boy. But those would be secondary effects. Honestly, I'd like to see my name in the *Free Press*, get paid to teach guerilla journalism, have a talking circuit, dispense my autodidactic experience. There would be no moon unless I needed a spotlight. I need to be universally loved...

Burns reenters, waving. His charisma disarms me. He seems like someone who can't compete with their own confession. I picture him on an operating table, demanding the surgeon hurry up. This city will see what I can do for it in his stead. Maybe he can be a career I drink myself through, the reflux of a better crime. The muscles in my face have grown sore from polite laughter.

On the ride home, singing the low parts of the Beach Boys, I'm pulled over. The two large officers who surround me appear more professional than is typical of the experience.

"Was I speeding?"

"You ask the wrong questions."

"Why not shoot me," I say, crossing my arms.

"No such luck today. Take my card." The one on the passenger side presents a middle finger. I let the world in slowly, magnet suction of a fridge door sailing shut.

"Want some beer?" I manage. The driver's-side officer is writing something down, I imagine an offer to help find the boy, with digits much richer than I'm prepared for.

"Make it a Blockbuster night, you shit." They walk away, laughing. I look at the piece of paper they handed to me.

Nothing about D'Wayne. Not even a code to decipher. It's just a traffic ticket.

My only hope is that my persistence does not end with being written on my face, but etches itself deeper, and is carved and imprinted, like a bullet making its cradle, in my skull.

EZRA'S HEAD

I give you your head, I fasten your head to the bones for you...
I split open your mouth for you, I split open your eyes for you

– Utterances 13 & 21, *Ancient Egyptian Pyramid Texts*
  (tr. R.O. Faulkner)

The dead are not all dead,
Myself I have returned

– Ezra Pound, Canto LXXIII

December

REDD BEYWARD chewed through his meditation cushion. "My miniature rebellion against this Whopper Jr. world!" he told the stuffing. A half-crazed girlfriend, whose mind had left her body to fend for itself, was the oasis of a singular thirst for him, so much so that he planned to line his innards with an entire pharmacy in her honor. His plan was as detailed as her newly institutionalized regimen.

Redd's backyard teemed with dead pets tucked a few feet beneath the turf, accumulating like the undigested pills would in his belly. Without her, Redd tore at his ugly stick-and-poke tattoos. Their legacy of mutual destruction was difficult to perpetuate by himself, though he continued to play the devil with some of their stranger occult obsessions, outwardly manifesting only in his incredible posture. He had trained his body, not unlike a dog, by wearing a rubber band around his wrist and snapping it against the skin whenever he noticed the beginning of a slouch.

He cataloged his crimes in verse, a line for each strap on her straitjacket. "The Prologue of the Unborn," his favorite, began like this:

> Into my loneliness comes a flute hole sharply
> Hacking back wildernesses never braved
> And I behold Pan
> His sky-wide nostrils eject the stars
> And his perfume smokes upwards to play me

Reciting the first stanza didn't bring a response from this or any other world. Redd cut his arm again, wishing Pan might groove some proxy to his nerves, or at least make an appearance to collect what he was owed. "The devil was our best idea," Redd decided, lying prostrate before paintings of the underworld. Classmates who knifed dirty words into the backs of school bus seats once brought tears to his eyes. He hated ever having done anything nice. "Nothing's worse!" he wept. For all the snot, tears, and semen adorning his pale body, its opacity did not increase. No dead jiggling breasts diminished the darkness of his room, mocking the liquid membranes magnified in his gaze. Redd was the type to race to the edge of sanity over a facial expression.

"But there is something worse," purred a voice behind the wall. Redd bowed over his clothes, yanking them clear. His nightmares had finally spoken their piece. Redd shut his eyes and kept silent the rest of the day, listening, ignoring the post-menopausal jailers upstairs. The flock of women he lived with had taught him how to lucid dream.

His Grandma Lori grew up when dollar bills and typewriters became credit cards and computers. It was no longer simple adverts in the Sunday paper detailing military advancements. Truckloads of machines were specified, built, and stacked into structures that rivaled Machu Picchu. The allure of the machines felt similar to an Incan citadel, although Lori could never comprehend the future archeology of her life. Men sparkling with sweat lugged contraptions that rinsed her clothes and dishes. Televisions guaranteed she'd stay up to date on the latest news, which was partitioned by advertisements for more technology. Appendages were added to the refrigerator to keep food fresher longer. Greens seemed forever crisp. She joked that she was finally a modern woman when her dangly sundresses snagged on the dishwasher's maw. Lately, she couldn't maneuver through the newfangled metal gate keeping her from wandering the street. It took a powerful thumb to unlock. Grandma Lori would wake Redd, shaking the bars, screaming at her daughter, Redd's aunt, "Casey, Casey! I need to take a bath! Let me out of here!" Beside the hospice bed taking up most of the room, every item in her chest of drawers lay buried beneath a row of diapers. Pride forced her to remain unsanitary. She pulled them up around her waist, in place of panties, whether they were empty or not.

Redd lumbered to the kitchen for a cup of coffee. Lori hunched over an enormous mug, stirring the spoon with both hands. She waited until his back was turned to speak: "Who will remember you when you're gone?" He chalked the vitriolic effrontery up to dementia. Her moods were sometimes expressed coherently enough to earn a violent response. Coffee stench mingled with ancient perfumes. The kitchen sank into itself. Wallpaper near the ceiling gathered perspiration, wrapping them in a flu-like skin. "Other people," he replied, in a baritone ill-suited for his sallow body.

"Exactly. That's why your opinion of yourself doesn't matter, except as a manipulation device to control others." Her dress was gold, brown, austere, and designed by someone French who Redd had never heard of. "What does that have to do with me?" Redd said, looking down at a full mug of coffee he had forgotten pouring.

"What did you think of me, growing up?" she asked, spoon clinking against a saucer.

"That you were a witch. That I should be afraid of you." Redd grew up submerged in cyclical dreams, which, due to the beliefs instilled in him, had meant too much. The logic of his waking life bred itself out of some nameless ether. Whenever he submerged his head in bathwater, the darkness behind his eyes munched closer.

In Redd's perennial dream, he was secured to a basement floor with thick gold chains. A hooded creature, so black it was silver, emerged from the dark. Redd began to levitate, strangled by the golden collar, and the creature nodded its head on a bony neck. Flaming doorways opened in a circle around them. Redd dragged his body by the chains, nearly snuffed of breath. He needed to trick himself into thinking he was just a man and not the devil this creature knew he was. Even if Redd believed psychiatrists did anything, he still wouldn't visit one.

Redd's Aunt Casey shoveled snow outside, blasting the Ramones, headbanging, limping between piles. A decade old self-inflicted gunshot wound slowed her chores. Last week, Redd had picked Aunt Casey up from a minor surgery to aid with her chronic pain.

"We're going to give you some pain medicine to take home with you. This one is called Norco," the nurse had said afterwards, like the pair of them didn't know what hydrocodone was, or why the acetaminophen was added to it: the liver could only handle so much Tylenol before it shut down.

"What are those, the ten milligrams?" Aunt Casey had said.

"No," the nurse said, with a sideways look, "they're the fives."

"Let's make 'em tens!"

"Well well well. We wouldn't want to make a junkie out of you, now would we?"

"Too late!" Aunt Casey said, slapping her knee.

In the kitchen, Lori flicked the pentacle dangling from Redd's neck. "You don't have to practice magic, Redd. Just manipulate people into thinking the banal things you do are miracles. People's lack of imagination fills in the rest."

Redd rolled his eyes and stumbled back to his cot, which was positioned in accordance with the earth's magnetism. In a feng shui book he'd stolen, north-facing headboards claimed to aid getting laid. He unrolled a bit of painter's tape and traced a five-pointed star above his bed, the peak aimed at his pillow. He called this his dream funnel. Don't angle the foot of the bed toward the door, he'd also read, as that's how a corpse is carried through the house—by its feet.

Grandma Lori died a week later, legs frozen crooked, rigor mortis stiffening the joints at an impossible geometry. Redd stared so woozily she appeared to breathe. The corpse was a creature that lacked boundaries. It stuck to one's sight. The nurse's aide had bathed her, but had not put her pajamas back on. Grandma Lori died wearing nothing but underwear. A thin window filled with condensation was the only thing between her frizzy black hair and Michigan's brutal winter. At first, the family draped a large green blanket over the body, but Redd's aunt decided to dress it before the men arrived. The green frock and black sweatpants were strangely difficult to put on, even though her body had shrunk. Redd felt coolness radiate from Grandma Lori's fingertips to her trunk. It was like trying to dress a wax doll whose elbows had melted into its torso.

"She'd be horrified if she saw us," Redd said.

"I just can't imagine her going out into the cold with nothing but underwear," Aunt Casey said. "I know it's nonsensical, but I feel very strongly about this." A chill remained in the house that evening, even with the thermostat cranked to 72 degrees.

Over breakfast the next morning—an Oats 'N' Honey granola bar and two mugs of Chock full o'Nuts—Aunt Casey confessed to Redd. "But you have to promise not to tell."

"Okay," Redd said.

"I've been getting messages," she looked down at the table, "I assume they're from God. Who else could they be from?"

Redd wondered if she wanted him to guess. He didn't tell his aunt about the voice he'd heard the other night. No reason to conflate mysteries. She spoke again, "I heard it last night when I was standing at the bathroom mirror. The air got really calm, as if I'd just taken my meds." She swallowed a deep breath, "but now that Mum's gone..." she trailed off.

"You don't think it was Grandma?" Redd said.

"No. It sounded the same as the voice that told me to take care of her."

"What'd it say?"

"That it's my turn. It also said to take you with me?"

"What does that mean?" Redd asked, frustrated with his aunt's upward inflection.

"I don't remember, it was late. You know I'd never

hurt you, I just wanted to mention it so you'd keep an eye out."

"When's the last time you used?"

"Don't," Aunt Casey said and pushed her chair out. "I didn't have to say anything. I weighed the options and figured it's better you knew."

Redd squinted, nodding condescendingly, and said, "How will I ever repay you?"

"Fuck off, Redd."

"Ah, not just a junkie, but a sailor too."

"I am what I am. Who would want more than that?" she said, descending the stairs, and then locked the door to her room. For whatever reason, to Redd, this was the final straw.

To kill himself, he gulped a cornucopia of barbiturates, chased by every ocean—first the Pacific, then the Atlantic—until what remained of the world was just a few square feet dried around him. With no help from physicians or family to make sure he didn't fall asleep before taking the number of pills needed to pause the lungs and stop the heart, Redd made damn sure his stomach was empty. The valve between his belly and the small intestine, where the magic happened, gasped every twenty seconds, and ushered in what he'd swallowed. The medicine rushed the small intestine with immediate effect. After swallowing all fifty pills in the bottle and lighting a cigarette, Redd tugged a plastic bag over his head and snapped rubber bands around his neck for good measure. He replayed his dreams with the captions on, strangely snoring as the drugs took over, unable to suck air through the plastic bags, until his heavy breathing stopped, the final exit came into view, and the ash fanned outward between his bagged lips, like a psoriatic arm reaching away, blooming...

January

THE WORLD appeared like bits of an apple spat back onto its core. A voice, jaunty with confidence, hovered everywhere.

"...he died more wretchedly than any man before him..."

"Here he comes. Something beneath a pittance." Another voice, female, full of British spite.

"Wait, this bitch ate the pills from his purse. No blood and thunder. We're not very well researched today..."

The three of them were just heads, floating a moment. "You are indirectly alive."

They had placed a helmet on Redd. Visors rose slowly, releasing a little peripheral vision. Darkness opened, beyond location, to faces nodding on an obelisk. Their platform glimmered. The back of his head felt sawed off.

"Did you imagine death would save you from your sentence? Did you think decay would spare you?"

Redd tried to scream, but could not situate a voice in his throat.

"I miss listening to them beg," one of the heads whispered.

Redd's nails felt chewed down by someone else's teeth, ripped to the joint, although he couldn't see his hands.

"You initiated death and it corrected what?" They seemed to be reading his mind. Redd tested a couple extraocular muscles, trying to locate the area's confines. At first he could only feel his eyes aching, burning, but then he noticed dozens of orbs shuffling below. The designs etched on the glowing helmets beneath him resembled snowflakes. Better to watch the snow melt on a jacket than to be caught in a museum, he had often thought. The clouds had more talent than anything alive. Suddenly, and perhaps accentuated by this unimaginable and ever-expanding pain, Redd felt extremely close to God.

"We will adjust this memory gone, but you tried killing yourself over a blonde? How the small of her back fit in your palm? The way her hair draped when she rode you?"

These memories felt squirted in via needle. He was being scalped from the inside. Rotten, deciduous teeth clicked down. Redd decided not to die again, even if he'd have to pull out each of those teeth, one by one. First he had to make himself move.

"You were nobody important. Not to be missed. Less than forgotten." The central head spun as if suspended on a globetrotter's finger. "Who's this nameless waste? Edward Derby?"

"No. Redd Beyward."

"Continue believing the propaganda that you only

live once, Beyward."

"He offed himself on schedule."

"Offed? As if consciousness could power down. Snap closed. A metamorphic moment that could bust the quotidian shut?"

One of the heads began nodding off.

"There is a place between heaven and earth, mostly theory. Every group that gathers to discuss us squeezes us out, flattens our bowels. No one can render the effect. We're the opposite of text. Delivered to those who deserve us."

"Even when our image is used to fan an agenda, the religious taxidermy of an idea, we avoid that ratty mascot suit."

Redd's temples throbbed, muscles of mastication sore beyond measure. A migraine ballooned from his neck until the air itself felt like a separate nerve ending getting scraped.

"We enjoy pitiful Buddhist theory for its widespread hells. Or how Americans believe they'll climb the vines of a dollar when they die, which is interesting."

Redd remembered being middle class, born without status into a family he could barely uphold. His disinterest in the lack of culture around him kept him in a continual pursuit of solace. Occultism skimmed close to what he thought, but veered away too dangerously. Emerging from the confines of these groups dislocated his empathy, the core of human nature erased, foundation free. Actions carried out as an aspiring Satanist reduced him to the opposite of what was promised. He was raw clay reshaped into nothing with the help of a hierophant. He thought that death might provide some relief, not produce more pain.

"Humans are either commercially viable, or treated like an enigma, if lucky. Try to describe the nothingness that you imagined would exist for you beyond the veil. We'll wait."

Mist hung on a river, cutting the grounds beneath them. Insectoid lightning strikes twitched in the clouds.

"...a species that spent its last mystery," a head droned on.

Had he only ever made an internal journey, a parallax scrolling of platforms disguised as one of many lives?

"Do you understand what it means to be named? When someone knows your name, they wield power over you. Once you know someone's name, you can make them do anything. The only name you deserve, however, is the sound of your own castration."

The creatures spoke themselves into a more mammalian shape. Under the drooling storm, they were no longer balls of light emanating from beyond. One appeared as a thin-legged giraffe wearing the face of Redd's father. The jaw kept falling off and had to be held in place with a hoof. Redd hadn't seen his father since he "vacationed" with a coworker years ago. He tried to forget about him, once shattering a mirror due to their resemblance. Personality, to Redd, seemed like a revolving door of many masks—try to clean them, but it's only a matter of time before they all come back around. This was no metaphorical death, like he'd practiced, changing pieces of himself here and there, whittling himself down, in search of his maskless self, his one true face. This was real.

The head in the center, their motor-mouthed overlord, morphed into a female commando shaped like Grandma Lori. He felt himself getting erect against his will. His will, what he believed to be his strongest attribute. The third head's neck grew in tandem, deepening its laughter aimed at Redd. Glyphs shifted from linear patterns, the resin of a contour. Some miniscule Ken doll of a man jumped up from the floor, grabbing and hanging from Redd's erection. The giraffe cut a bleeding slit in Redd's jeans, unfolding the rest of his scrotum with an X-Acto knife, zip-tying the entirety, tightening it until the glans throbbed horribly purple, a chapped flap vacuumed of moisture...

Redd bounced and jerked as if riding inside a carriage car. His immobile body had returned and it sagged like dead weight in a hospital bed beneath him. He grasped the hand next to him in bed. The hand was stiff and freezing. He dropped it and tried to sit up. There were others like him: strapped to beds, bodies jostling with the movement of the room, groins wrapped in bandages that didn't fully mop the mess. A creature as long as a piece of string wrapped itself around a lever above his bed, tugging downward, asking for help. Redd tried flashing a polite smile, but every time he formed an expression, his lips slid off his face. He reached toward the creature, past the sopping wet bandage, then lost consciousness...

The heads were back, Redd beneath the helmet, no body to be seen. His lips were soldered shut by a chemical cocktail. He looked down at the ox bones dangling from his neck. They'd been sculpted into a rosary of human skulls. No chant could help him. These floating heads read his thoughts like braille.

"Nothing but destruction in your songbook." The head shaped like his grandmother was reverse-aging. Where his body was resembled an early PlayStation game, a perspective with no internal structure built into the code.

"The scientific obsession with molecular biology infiltrates us with a new guilt, beyond Christianity, for ready-made structures. There's a famous statue of Shiva, crescent moon on his forehead, thousands of feet tall, facing the ocean, representing the gap between humans and gods. Easier to bow to the statue itself than anything it might be thinking. To make destruction your tradition. No more blowup doll Madonnas."

Perhaps this was Redd's second, final death. The lake of fire had rental arrangements with every religion.

"Did you install the latest updates?" This was

directed to someone behind Redd. The sky revealed itself apart from nature, the two moving in distinct directions, spinning about some yellow globule. Trees were injected with Botox to smooth their bark. Gears and conveyor belts lapped seamlessly around him, without sound, without operators. The three heads floated again behind their obelisk. Severed body parts dropped onto the belt. Everything except a head.

"Virginia, darling, fix his shit." One of them was falling asleep again, mumbling under a gigantic book with *One Must Be Extraordinarily Modern* written on the spine. Redd recalled how the modernists had a fixation on remixing the old, making it new. A library backdrop flickered. Of course in hell they'd turn his favorite locations against him.

"Virginia? Would you take care of... what's his name?"

"This won't hurt," a voice crooned. The head they'd called Virginia selected a disembodied torso and a pair of legs off the belt and situated them next to Redd. She caught fluids dropping from their stitches in the upside-down helmet that she'd peeled off of Redd's head. The black material under them was decorated with the handprints of ghosts. Moisture from each passing hand vanished.

"We try to sync everything up the first time, but sometimes we get it wrong. It's an arbitrary practice, like pop art."

Silos in the sky opened on an explosion already taking place.

February

REDD TRIED to wince back into his coma. Gathered about the hospital bed, family members caught him peeking. He wanted to take a pair of pliers to the sight of them. Every smidge of light entered his head and fractured it closer to zero. His organs wrung out the rest, distended belly of the globe mocked by the sun's malnourishment. He was returning to a surveillance state. Some out-of-state aunt addressed Redd. A nurse bit the curtain in solidarity.

He'd been out for a week. In another, they said he might be up and walking. His vitals were stable, but he'd needed transfusions. The pills had ruined his gut. The nurses explained Crohn's disease: fungi, viruses, bacteria in revolt, a system in overdrive now on slightly less harmful biologic drugs. Whether the chronic illness was a side effect of his suicide attempt or merely an underlying condition they couldn't say. It would be a glass-coated unit until his body responded, and pharmaceuticals all the way to death.

The curled and sticky wound across his belly stank like an autopsy. The smell resided with him, beneath all the sterilizers and ointments, almost sanitary. Counting sheep to beeps, hums, and drones, he saw each machine as a glowing orb hooked to veins, wire supplementation, a catheter choked down his cock and wended round a parabola, dripping inside a container. The backs of both hands were taped, receiving fluids. An empty port sat near his elbow waiting to be used. A thin tube edged food through his stomach. Every nasogastric head movement felt like a fork to the tonsils. Bowel prep slid in the tube, alongside food-like substances that tested his stomach's reach. He drowned in Jell-O in his dreams. Offered a straw to breathe, he sucked deeply, but there was only more jam.

They waited, leaning in, to see if his bowels would evacuate. They were going to pass his shit around the staff. Nothing would come. His stomach bloated. Still hungry, he gnawed their pap. Undissolved honey sat at the bottom of his black tea. Either his flimsy stirrer would melt in the hot liquid and become ineffective or the tea was too cold to absorb the honey. Redd was also miserably refusing to integrate.

The male nurse who came to clean Redd called himself Ken. Ken liked opera. Not even live opera. He had huge hands and his huge white hair got everywhere. "Foam in, foam out," he joked. Everyone was a lunch lady petting Redd to death. Having one's privates ground clean by another grown man was a new silent humiliation, a preview of old age, zero dignity daily.

Ken sprayed blue foam across Redd's ass, sopping the small puddle of blood in which his testicles floated.

Blood loosed anally in a steady stream. It was too early for stool to form, so it drizzled out like an open wound. He felt like a middleman for the diet they subjected him to. He was internally bleeding from meal to meal, fed more blood thinners than calories, and nurses worried less about him bleeding out than his legs clotting. Large white cuffs, encircling both calves, were squeezed symmetrically to simulate walking.

"Why they ain't workin'," some nurse spat, pumping bags of refrigerated blood into the large ports on the backs of Redd's hands. Temperature, like everything else, behaved strangely as Redd's hands felt like they were on fire. Another nurse corrected her, said something about one bag at a time, but neither of them pinched the line or adjusted the flow. Complaints, compliments, and adjustments to the invisible doctor's orders—everything went ignored.

Redd was sweating in the winter cap they'd put on him. Perhaps he would never shower again. He nearly asked for a mirror because the faces his relatives made made it feel like he was visiting his own wake.

"Take him off them thinners," his Aunt Casey commanded.

"But—"

"Don't care," she snapped. The bleeding did halt a day later. Rocks in his abdomen were being shaped by an erosion of blood. On the tiny TV above the hospital bed, the rest of the family watched the Tigers.

After this vomit-scented stint, he was delivered by force to the psychiatric wing. Redd was turning green under a different fluorescent. Pimples swelled on his itching nose. He had earned the pity and disgust of women before, but never in such measures.

Too fatigued to hide his meds, he took them. Posters rotated with black, white, and Mexican children holding hands atop the globe. A lithe woman, shy of eighty pounds, stared at Redd, mouth whisperingly ajar. He approached to hear her. She was so thin she could have hidden in the shadow of a shadow.

"...no different than anyone else's story. It all started during the war."

Redd tried to disrupt her chatter: "Are you lost?"

The woman scratched a raw wound on her arm. "I'm not a junkie," she hissed.

A man on the couch behind them was grinding his teeth and snorting. They listened to him for a minute. The man ripped stuffing from the cushion between his legs and tossed it into the air.

"You have nice hands," Redd told her eventually.

The folds of her thighs draped over the chair like cooked chicken.

"A guy I knew painted my hands once," she said. "He said I had the most beautiful hands ever. It's a common theme, men informing me of the legendary prowess of my hands. But they're not nice anymore. They're all crunchy. Soon as I started shucking corn and washing dishes, they were over."

"Crunchy?"

"Layers of dryness."

"Really?" Redd was getting hard for the first time in a while.

"Last week the roach people came and sprayed. Dead bodies everywhere. They made us stay in the kitchen while they worked. Then I had to sweep them all up. It took hours. My hands are still kind of blistered from the broom."

There was a streetlight directly outside Redd's bunk. He had the room to himself. A cage separated patients from the window. Below, cell phone cords, stripped wires, and leaves swirled in reverse. At breakfast, Redd was too tired to talk to the woman. Instead, he sat at a table where everyone was over fifty.

"It got grapes, green grapes," someone said.

"You tried it?" another one.

"That's why I 'int get none." There were five of them chatting like this. How all these patients knew each other was beyond him. Like he'd stumbled back into that realm of severed heads.

"Ever go to Sylvia's in Harlem?"

"Yeah."

"Still livin' when you went there?"

"She got two words: good 'n quiet."

"Tastes like a carmel apple." It did taste like a carmel apple, this thing that Redd had scraped out of a large silver tray over which everyone was slobbering.

"I took mine back to the hotel."

Redd guessed that they were back to talking about Sylvia's.

"You did?"

"He was drunk, he didn't know what he was doin'."

"We went to a seafood restaurant and had a po boy."

"New Olands."

"New Orlands."

"Nolands."

"Naw lans."

Then one of them spelled it, "N-A-W-L-A-N-S," and they all laughed.

"And they had those shotgun houses you just look straight through."

"I think a lot of those places were destroyed."

"Just this last week, New Orleans has been hit hard."

"Yeah."

"Tornadoes, man."

"Yeah."

"Well then a flood this time."

"Yeah."

"It's sin city, man." The tall guy was looking around to see if he could get a chuckle. Redd flashed him a smile so that he'd keep going.

"They say a hundred tornadoes touched down, man."

"Now how in the hell—"

"And they never rebuilt from the other part."

"No, they didn't."

"Mm-mm."

"That's sin city, mane, all those sex shops and that. That's the lord smiting."

The carmel apple dish was gone, and with it the nodding, fingerlicking, and toothpicking.

Redd's roommate returned from solitary, stinking and talking to ants. "Only way to stay sane," he said. He had shit himself to prove a point. When the roommate nodded off, Redd stretched his legs and snuck into a hallway occupied by cameras that no one seemed to be actively watching. He knocked on the girl's room. She blushed and issued a muffled yelp as he eased the door open and twisted the knob to silence it shutting. His father had had a temper and Redd learned to piss quietly in the night.

"One of the guards let me borrow her phone to watch Netflix with," the woman droned.

"That's nice."

"There's this show, I can't believe it's on my screen. *Book Sellers.*"

"Okay."

"These people are searching for vintage books. They got walls full. They don't read 'em. It's just an obsession. Some are as big as that table. Pages you have to turn with both hands."

Redd reached for the phone.

"Get your own!" She shoved him off the bed a little.

"Wait," Redd hushed. "Can I tell you a secret?"

"Yeah," she whispered.

"When I was in college, I watched that Pink Floyd movie *The Wall* a lot. Remember when those vagina flowers devoured the male flowers...?"

"Kind of."

Redd had been with an entire spectrum of men and women, but it was always the same. He had never told anyone how much he wanted to be brutalized so that he could retaliate. Though he'd tried: the last dominatrix he invited over flinched when given directives. Genuine confession would have to do. He couldn't hurt himself, or someone else, enough otherwise. Looking back on his past thirty years of what everyone around him called a life, he felt a similar disgust that he did when naked with another person.

"I used to be friends with this girl named Edith," the woman offered. She went on and on about her friends, some of whom she'd lost touch with, others who were dead.

Redd was pretty sure she wasn't responding to what he'd said, certainly not to what he'd hinted at, but was satisfied with paying attention to where her ass was on the mattress, glad to have kept his mouth shut.

"I don't think people understand," she said. "Of course we end up in here." She was crying now. Redd didn't have a clue. The puddle reached his shoulder.

The girl was a black hole. The farther away from her he walked, the less of an effect on him she had. He left her sobbing beneath that impossibly dotted ceiling. He would do everything in his power to get, and stay, out of there forever. He pretended that his paranoia could be stuffed deep into his pockets like his cigarettes, said all the magic words, and was gone in less than a week.

March

REDD'S VISION went analog. His frozen fingers tingled then approached a place beyond sensation. Bumped about inside pulsating organs, a ghost haunting his own skin, Redd felt like a surgeon standing over himself, fiddling in the open cavity. He occluded one nostril and palmed snot. Wind from the window chilled everything around him. He had escaped the lemon-scented products that had hovered above his hospital bed. It was nice when the mucus didn't leave a trail. Waddling fat kin with automotive microbiomes often would. Redd hit the knob on the dash.

...time is 9:58, traffic and weather together on the eights from the Bill Brown Ford Traffic Center: We're looking at post-Tigers traffic on westbound 94, slow after

M-59, and there's a crash that's taking up the left lane on northbound 75, looks like you're backed up from before 696 all the way back to the Boulevard, so avoid that area if you can. Let's go now to our resident meteorologist Virginia Woolf. Hi Leo... zzzzz

...The time is now ten o'clock, get started at James McNeill Whistler dot com. It really is important to know that you are not feeling so well, and just know that there is always something wrong with seeking help... zzzzz

...Execution's scheduled for 11 p.m., but he's trying to convince us he's gone insane... and therefore incapable of being executed... I need you to prove he's fakin' it... Edward, I'm gonna ask you some questions... I'm not Edward, I am a demon... Give me something to make me believe... I will inhabit you... Do you believe in the devil?... I can't stop him... Help me!... It doesn't matter what you believe... It can go away... How?... It's starting to happen... Names are important... Can you feel it?... It's time to face... Your demons... I think it's time we tell you exactly what it is we'd like you to do... zzzzz

Bodycam footage was just released from the Detroit bank rampage. As police raced to the scene at the corner of Mound and Twelve Mile... We do have numerous weapons recovered from the vehicle... Eventually the copycat gunman was shot and killed. This is the third such incident this week in the vicinity. The all-clear was given earlier today at the 36th District Courthouse following a bomb threat this afternoon. Right next to Ford Field. Police are telling WWJ that they don't think these two events are connected, but that everyone should be on the lookout for more copycat killers...

Redd parked, turned the keys, clicks from the handbrake yanked his spine straight. Menthol air sucked each lung in, not enough to cough.

He reached for the key, lanyard flopping. The door was locked, but not fully shut. Knob gripped, he keyed back and forth. It slid the rest of the way ajar. The stairway to his aunt's flat stank like garlic. Bangladeshi neighbors downstairs. The Kenyans next door screamed as if he was the source of their pain. The Poles one over were still breaking their pit bull pups, night after night. The stairs croaked beneath Redd like frogs in hell. He wanted to eat his earplugs.

Hamtramck was a city lost inside a bigger city. Even the homeless were confused. Their fungal, punctured skins sawed them off the map. Abandoned banks and libraries similarly became dead produce even gnats rejected. The sign of a long-downed meat factory still glowed bright pink. The stores all had bulletproof glass. He was going to smoke again.

He picked at the pack's silver guts. The chemicals in his tobacco reached a sharper precipice than before. Redd stepped onto the balcony and lit a cigarette. This was where Aunt Casey said that she had found him having his non-epileptic seizure. Once she ripped off the bag, she'd found off-white foam floating between his lips. Emergency technicians couldn't fit their gurney up the narrow set of stairs. They cradled him, she'd said, to the ambulance in a sheet, smashing his head on the cement. His government-supplemented insurance refused to pay for this. Several dialysis treatments stripped the lithium from his blood. This heavy metal mood stabilizer had been ingested in toxic quantities. He was, by their own admission, "lucky" to be alive. Redd thought of the dream he'd had of the severed heads, the horrifying sensations he'd undergone there, and hated that those idiots were right. Not because life was grand, but because death was a nightmare. Sadly, it was better to be alive.

Every day the sky turned schizoid colors, a primordial soup of unfulfilled tornado warnings. Redd dressed the same in every weather. Even his boxers were black. Upon entering the Fisher Building, one would first notice that the three-story barrel-vaulted lobby had been ornately painted. Ancient golden doors swayed, opening unto magnificent frescoes of Aztec-themed birds of prey, mythic cherubs, and gilded palms. The arcade was adorned with forty different kinds of marble. Birds fluttered around the second and third stories. The four-hundred-and-forty-one-foot skyscraper was considered to be Detroit's largest art object.

Redd worked in the theater, tucked into the heart of the first floor of the Fisher Building. First he filled an ice bucket. His bacterial issues went unmentioned. He would make use of their private restrooms.

"Open bar tonight," Redd's boss said, popping out from his hiding spot behind a gigantic fake banana tree, face glowing from the upward angle of his phone.

"Who's doing food?" Redd asked. The girl who brought the food out from the back was cute. Redd tried remembering her name. In the darkness between shows, roaches found the snacks. The building was over a century old. The bugs had been there longer. Employees knew not to leave their bags on the ground, but today the popcorn and gummy bears were pristine, as if something had frightened the pests.

Lucious McVay, daddy to thousands, father to none, laid prone upon the ground. "Waiting on the devil," he told his imaginary imp. The Nain Rouge was a red imp who tunneled from the earth's core, a hobgoblin whose appearance presaged misfortune, his elven ears like lean-tos for his beard. McVay only removed his Stetson to press closer to the floor. McVay could hear the devil in the globe, traumatizing her. The screams below reminded him of his sisters playing church organs. They all gathered in the pit to sing.

McVay had taken an Uber on his sister's dime, and promised the driver a basket full of stars. Broken Styrofoam gathered beneath his boots. Over the span of one breath, a ground-down cigarette butt burnt down to its cotton filter. The glass door emblazoned with gold got caught on its decade-old hinges as he tugged it open. He whiffed stale air. Cable boxes hummed in the walls, electric wires burped, flickered out. There was a pause before the world started back up again. For bystanders, it was impossible to ignore the large man barreling through the arcade. For McVay, there was only one soul that stank like an escaped reincarnation. He followed the scent down into the lounge, where he'd be meeting his sister. His boots clicked closer to the young man, his charge.

"Welcome," Redd said. "Have you been to the Fisher Lounge before?"

"First time," McVay spat, gold teeth grinning.

As Redd spieled about the private restrooms, he saw that the man's nametag stitched across the heart of his mechanic's uniform said "Lucious." Redd glanced back at his liquor steps to see how much cognac was left. Jazz shows like these brought a mostly black audience. Some assumptions had to be made. McVay's sister soon joined him. She enjoyed a different drink with each trip to the bar, tipping pleasantly. McVay didn't tip. The drip of ice into the plastic bucket beneath the cooler was hard to unhear once Redd heard it. Redd's sweat pushed through the deodorant. A decent perfume would have harmonized such an affront.

Redd hustled drink orders to and from the cash register, smiling hellishly. Not long ago, rain had seeped its way down to this lower level. They refurbished everything. People rode jet skis over the streets of Hamtramck. Freeways were swimmable. Every parked car had its engine engulfed.

The dead pit bull Redd passed on his way to work had vanished after the deluge. He missed seeing her, and wondered what dimension she had ended up in.

"You look like you in your twenties," McVay said, ordering more cognac.

"Worse." Redd had never cut someone off before. He scooped fresh ice.

"By the time you forty, I want you to do betta," McVay said, grinning. A man standing next to him let the teeth drop free from his head. Perturbed about candy fish prices, he insisted on catching some walleye and perch himself. Redd laughed, politely. Dozens of gnats played Ring Around the Rosie at the bottom of the bottle of Jack. The playlist of jazz standards cycled.

"Lemme get a scrap of paper," McVay said. Under the bent letters of his name he scrawled a number, dropping it next to someone's wife's purse. The woman blushed.

"Pick that up," McVay's sister said.

"Pick what up?" McVay said, playing dumb.

"You embarrassing her. Pick it up."

McVay did, unfolded it, slapped it against the counter, and stared at Redd. The eyes beyond bloodshot, their corners curled up into smiles.

A woman walked toward the bar done up in black and gold. Artistically shaped braids. She ordered fancy drinks and namedropped Chaka Khan.

"She grabbed me right back like we were sisters!" she yelled, sliding a five across the bar before heading to the restroom.

"That a bitch or a nigga?" McVay slurred. "You hear what I said?" He had pretended to search the room before asking, but several other customers were within earshot. Still, he leaned in and said, "Only one way to find out, cuz I only do pussy." Redd blushed.

After sweeping, mopping, and picking up their junk, Redd and his coworkers didn't get to the parking garage until well past ten. The Nissan's engine turned over, warmly. He called his ex to hear her voicemail. McVay's complaints played through his brain.

McVay tested the wind with his finger. He felt the boy's soul squeezed and wetted as if compressed between two microscope slides.

Horribly shaped groins began leaking.

With his post-surgical bacterial infections—Vibrio cholerae and Clostridioides difficile (more commonly known as C. diff)—Redd Beyward was an easy host for demonic entry. The bacteria in Redd's bowels worked like commas: jerky, confused. Rain turned to hail and sounded like knocks coming from inside the coffin.

A draft from Redd's century-old window gave rise to the scrap of paper with McVay's number on it. Redd's hand curled into a claw and the paper danced and melted like snow inside the globe of his paw as he slept.

April

EVERY DAY juxtaposed hot and cold. Facebook boomer selfies were posted in the snow. They commented: "April showers!" Furnaces and air conditioners alternated hourly. Redd hit remission with drink and drugs. He felt bellied by the night. A short waitress at the bar touched her tattoos. They couldn't fuck unless she somehow hid those fingers. Each fat nail had been chewed to the blood-grooved cuticle and remained unwashed. Two-Beer Tommy, a ceramicist ten years sober, choked down a Guinness. The wooden table seemed handcrafted until an object was set on it.

"You're more in your art now." Redd pointed at Tommy's stained clothing.

"People censor themselves by getting dressed."

Redd's female friend appeared, completing a cocaine maneuver between the bathroom and her nose. Random goodwill occurred more often when she slinked around in half her clothes.

"Guess her weight," Tommy said.

"Too much?" Redd said.

"You, meanwhile, shrank to the size of AIDS."

"Good thing I only come when the condom breaks."

The house looked blurred out by the party inside. A Motown mansion repurposed by yuppies. Redd entered discussions with a number of mustachioed men. A girl passed by, hair squeezed up so hard her head was bleeding. Otherwise pasty and bored, she sported some maniacal bangs. Redd followed her and her cigarette outside, moving a lighter towards both. She used just her eyes to look. Two orange circles passed between them in the dark. They were tapping patterns across the wooden slats. She parted mid-small talk. Redd paced the property line. The air was getting dense. Something scarier than fog. His stomach hurt, sharp pain in the upper left side. Beer carbonation maybe helped. He wanted to stab a partygoer.

Redd's ex had left him for a schizophrenic. The idiot stood there now, wearing a cape, eyebrows freshly shaved, stack of library books on a string he kept retying. A collarless dog presented itself.

"Don't pet that dog!" the schizophrenic hissed.

"Why the fuck not?"

"Stroke that dog from neck to tail and it'll begin to seizure."

"Oh," Redd patted the head. The head nudged for more, looking sad. Redd was close to smearing its coat with spit. The looney had carefully placed the ember of his cigarette in his mouth and was blowing a cloud of smoke out the butt, cross-eyed, watching his own party trick. Men with faces painted like cats pranced around and meowed.

Everyone's tight clothes made Redd itch. Couples could trace the placement of their limbs as the dance progressed.

Bangs girl poked Redd's waist, fished through his pocket, and typed him her number. Mostly gays were left. A nude woman on top of the refrigerator swiped at passersby. He tilted about the party, sniffing participants. They moved like they were all caught in the same doggy door. A tall man wore a top with no bottoms. His shriveled dick sprang inward. Redd drew imaginary lines between the two of them and the moon, then imagined using that sharpened triangle to cut off the man's head.

That night a stitched bulge emerged under the skin of Redd's lower right abdomen. He probed the obtrusion, imagining people at the party trapped in there, screaming for air. Imagining bangs girl at waist height and out of breath was enough for Redd to get himself off once, which helped the bloated feeling, and briefly relieved some anxiety, which he'd noticed only after chewing through his cheek until he tasted blood.

The neighbor looked like he was doing some kind of Gitmo yoga over his mower, as if the tortuous bend of his body was aiding in priming the machine for the season. Dogs chased the rake across the lawn. A bird made machine-gun sounds. Redd was hungover. The calendar blurred. Two-Beer Tommy's geologist dad was having a funeral. The ice age of religiosity was warming over into one great indulgence. The brand of Satanism everyone he knew practiced was called "Esoteric Satanism." Redd didn't really think the devil flew about at night, but the image moved him.

"What do you guys believe?" Redd remembered asking. The air was freezing, and his fingers had gone numb in the tips of his gloves.

"We don't make anyone believe in anything they don't want to," the group had said. "We don't force anything on anybody. We pride ourselves in being very open."

Perhaps this should have worried Redd, but at the time it comforted him. What he wanted was a group of people as interested in the occult as he was.

Bright yellow forsythia blooms had spread across the grass like a rash. No herbicides for the dandelions either. The city gave him more and more insects. Windshield wiper fluid merely smeared their insides. The town center sat around a single statue. Several turkey vultures' short ivory-colored beaks glimmered in the sun, then the birds turned to look at Redd. He abandoned his vehicle in the loop. Cars honked and circled to honk at him again. It was one of the strangest things Redd had ever seen. Awake, anyway. That is, if he was awake. (And here he was heading to a wake. And to make matters worse, a group of feeding vultures was known as "a wake"—but he shook off this linguistic syzygy because he wanted to experience the conjunction of the turkey vultures and the sculpture.) Approaching the statue, Redd saw that it was an artistically rendered human head with holes in the mandible, more intricate designs inside, other heads like eggs grown within the copper shell. Two turkey vultures spread their wings, bright red faces craning, seeming to pay obedience to the bronze sculpture. Like the turkey vultures' septumless noses, the statue had a tunnel leading to the second half of the sculpture. Another vulture was squeezed into another opening, hissing and grunting at Redd as he approached. A copse of trees obscured the other side. The statue was two halves split down the middle, dizzyingly. Redd figured that he'd keep a bald face too if he had to chew through gaseous roadkill.

Redd drove to the service, parking on a hill. He had driven with the parking brake engaged so many times he wasn't sure it worked, though he pulled it anyway, just for fun. Weepy groupings swooped near Two-Beer Tommy. Redd told them it was nice to meet them too many times. Three grandkids in the front row disrupted the service. He saw one spit blood. Afterward, an aunt and uncle of Tommy's across the room distracted him from a parental line of questioning.

"Has Tommy convinced you to move to California yet?" the aunt said.

"No, I love Michigan actually. I'll be here my whole life," Redd said.

"Oh. I've never heard that before."

"Yeah, I love it here."

"What do you love about it?"

He couldn't tell if it was the way it was asked or if maybe he didn't love it as much as he claimed, because he felt defensive and he couldn't think of anything. He stalled.

"What do they call it again?" the aunt startlingly asserted.

"Sorry, what?" Redd said.

"Don't they call this the Blue State? Like California is the Golden State, you know? Michigan, yeah, I think they call it the Blue State."

"I've never heard of that."

"What do *you* call it?" she said.

"The Great Lake State?" Redd was annoyed.

"No," she eructed, conferring with a daughter, who silently agreed with Redd, then a husband.

"Hell, I don't know what they call it, why don't you ask him!" the husband said, pointing at Redd. "This guy lives here for Christ's sake."

"You mean Pure Michigan?" Redd tried.

"Jesus, yes! And isn't it pure? We saw the lakes, flying in. So blue," she trailed off.

Redd excused himself to shit.

May

"**H**OW CAN someone so sexy be so messed up inside? So sick that their own beauty becomes an afterthought? It'd be a shame to live in another body tonight, to depart from the afterbirth of beauty scratched out by better trained men, these autistic butchers who need to deprive me of my grave because they are not sensual enough to mend much beyond everyone's inner fixings."

Redd had recovered at Aunt Casey's, enduring such thoughts. Projected over his squeezed-shut lids was a Polaroid of himself from the nuts up, wrenching them to and fro, whispering, like the shudder of a fortune teller: "Is this your card, is this your card...?"

He called the offices of many doctors, tongue retreating

from mouth to throat. Nurses ordered blood samples. Grinning phlebotomists tugged needles down his arm as if they meant to trample an insect beneath a rug. He lost weight on purpose, afraid of the stools they'd take.

To worsen his outcome, he ate at diners. The regular deaf patron would squeak when he signed. Redd had learned his friendliest gestures: "what's up," "how are you," et cetera. Bangs girl practiced signals in bed. Her stupid name was Heaven. She doted over an alcoholic father's threats. They were at her squat overhearing loud friends. Thrifty farmers gave them room and board if labor was performed sunup till sundown. Heaven filled the field with piss and shit. Everyone unknowingly loved her nutrients. The whole world had a preference for social justice. Her creativity came out in her tan. But the sex was regular, and this lulled Redd into considering moving here.

"The idea of the zombie ant fungus is also gaining popularity," Redd reiterated whenever she bored him with her views.

"Maybe ants like dying under orders, high up in the wind," she peeped. "I need to know the right amount of secrets about you so I can accuse you of something later."

"You know Bob Flanagan? The supermasochist? His motto was: 'fight sickness with sickness.'"

"Where's your secret?"

"BDSM," he almost yelled, picturing each letter as a latex balloon filling her unfinished loft. "Let's indulge."

"What's the safe word?" she said, propped on elbows, head tilted.

"The sound of a well-drawn breath blown up inside a pregnant woman's vulva, which is rumored to result in death."

Redd stirred dried blue lotus flower into a twenty-dollar bottle of wine, potentiating the herb. They drank their horny syrups together and lit candles, Throbbing Gristle blaring. She removed filthy cloth panties. Redd dripped wax across her belly, shaped it in her pubic hair. She stank like cut grass. Sharp-angled shadows filled the room. Redd pressed her down. The harder he pressed, the more they felt like they were floating.

"Ouch!" Heaven said. Redd stopped, tasted blood, unsure whose. "That hurt."

"Sorry," Redd said. Her silhouette shrank back into shadow, and she covered her mouth in the wake of a passionate kiss.

"Let's take a break," she said through her hand, consonants muffled.

When Redd was growing up, hand signs for the deaf were printed across his school playground. He saw them change in every dream. Redd felt like he was coming out of anesthesia.

Effort with a fucked body proved difficult. Luckily, trying was still uncool. He canceled his accounts—social media and otherwise. Aunt Casey kept herself perpetually drugged, experiencing Branch Davidian apocalyptic visions. She saw the cult's children writhing in the fire, playing AC/DC's "Burnin' Alive" on a loop. The food in her fridge provoked her diabetes. Athletic armbands, originally purchased with their intended use in mind, now covered a constellation of collapsing veins. The government paid her something near a grand a month. What she didn't spend on smack she used to purchase VHS tapes on eBay, stacked floor to ceiling. With every click of her computer mouse, Aunt Casey's belly grew. The house shrank around them both, much like Redd's intestine slowly scarring itself shut.

Redd was ready to move in with Heaven, but had to wait out an infected bowel. It was quite contagious, Clostridioides difficile, also known as C. diff. He aimed to maintain his rare diseases well. Burger King was hiring. Disinfecting the toilet seat and sink after each restroom visit—not bleach, but soap and water—flattered the thing's reach. Now he only knew Aunt Casey by the occasional click of a rice cooker and spared her the worry. A fat guy entered the residence to fuck her sometimes, a sound above demolition. Redd had C. diff, cholera, vibrio, E. coli. "No problem, really," he told people. "Mostly kills the old." He'd die thin, if not young.

Redd often wondered about species of insects that thrived in extreme environments, and how humans had mostly gravitated toward comfort. Temperature regulation, soft clothes, pleasant dreams, pain reduction, plain language, clean air: it goes to show that not all life forms are created equal and that if certain species can live on the edge of a volcano and others on pitch-black vents at the bottom of the sea then those of us who need so much of what sculpts us eliminated to live should give up the reins.

According to Redd's phone, his ex was leaving the asylum soon. Intimacy had been her only taboo, diddled in the crib. He helped her get over her issues to the best of his ability—sometimes by pretending to be the father or brother that she never had when they fucked—and she clawed him, which he liked.

"Abuse survivors are drawn to the occult," Heaven said whenever he ranted about his ex.

"You're referring to the psychosomatic astrology accusation that under-experienced medicines trot out," he said, giving her the middle-finger signal. "You're the kind of bitch who never plays victim hard enough. Quote me more borrowed thoughts." He cut himself so she could see, for emphasis.

"We need to talk," she said.

"Jesus," he said.

"We're sort of in an open relationship, right?"

She would text him lines like "I carry unborn worlds around with me." To this he would reply, "I love you," then deeply regret it. They were already fucking to the wub of the ceiling fan.

She explained how her ex-boyfriend, the chef, was no longer leaving for Thailand to study the culinary arts. They should officially open their relationship to accommodate him. Redd pictured his ex dropping a cell phone down the front of her straitjacket, then letting him fish it out. The idiot before him continued: "Lovers should be more like friends. Friends more like lovers."

"Jesus," Redd said when she finished. "How about we take a break. Like on that show everyone like you likes."

Heaven complained about Redd's temper. Maybe she'd do better being trafficked through a series of Thai kitchens. Redd decided to move to the farm anyway, just to spit in her crops.

June

T HE DIRT lot was sprinkled with just enough gravel to make walking barefoot a pain. A Ken doll of a man, his happy trail widening where jeans thankfully took over, was the only occupant of the dirt lot when Redd arrived at the farm. Propped under a car hood, he barred the path to a barn that looked like it'd been built by the dead. Redd had been granted zero access. Too much machinery loomed inside, tools with rusted edges. He would go on to remain an intern. The farmers said that Redd would be learning, but really it meant that they needn't pay him much. He did, however, become less and less iffy with a stirrup hoe. The Ken doll frowned as if he might shit what he said next.

God was squatting over a cloud to turn it pink. Redd could mentally populate several sci-fi landscapes before this guy issued word one. Although when Redd asked the Ken doll about Heaven (Redd gestured with his hand to imitate her bangs), the guy replied, "Oh, she's gone."

Heaven had lured Redd to the farm, claiming not to get along with anyone else, but really, Redd thought, she probably wanted a proper shower. He hoped he'd never cross paths with her again.

Nothing was a matter of will anymore. Redd could break his body to make it sleep and build it back in dreams. All the rooms of the shack where he lived were inhabited. Another Midwestern hovel. People stared without waving. Behind a rag-sized wall, Suzie, this writer girl with an appetite, announced herself repeatedly. Her bobbed hair, barely influenced by the breeze, stuck to the chocolate around a single sucked finger. She kept her distance.

Redd's car had a broken muffler. The rattle comforted him. It sounded like the patronizing advice of a neighbor. He drove it to and from town, oftentimes with unshowered coworkers nestled in the backseat. Redd's ex, wherever she was, perhaps being butterfly-netted, let her current schizoid boyfriend practice yoga in crowded areas, which Redd observed once at the local bookstore in town. Redd wasn't well-trained enough to interest an idiot. Before the ex was hauled away, Redd came in her socks and she put them back on anyway. The distance in these instances was agreeable. Now his colleagues were stooping in the field, paddling through vegetation. They wore hats of a questionable size. No phones, no chatter. They were even free of passing formalities. Rebellions against their suburban American upbringing manifested in unanswered sneezes. Redd would sneeze for three months without ever being blessed or saluted. He wanted inside that barn.

Before he left for the summer, Aunt Casey had tried dissuading him. Redd missed only the cleanliness of tending bar.

"Let's play the presidents game," she'd said.

"What?"

"Rank the presidents of the United States. You go first. Go on."

Redd had needed a break from this house, from his aunt. He would, in fact, go all the way out of the city. Aunt Casey's tank top seemed chewed up and spat back on her body. There were wind chimes he'd planted outside, soon to be so tangled they'd never touch, abandoned. Aunt Casey wanted an excuse to rant about the reigning president. Redd feigned ignorance of the man's name. They both had blue squares of painter's tape covering their phone cameras. She smiled when Redd took his one uninsured opiate.

On his drive to the farm, the news said they were grooming children to become lifelong Tigers fans. Most of what Redd claimed to think, he imagined, was a product of advertisements. He asked the car radio if it would please stop.

The farm dog's big walloping heart was tangible when it laid on people. If Redd dared to touch his toes, his frontal and maxillary sinuses became plugged. The dog snored, eyes at a jot. He pictured the animal's dream: food source of his own caught prey, finished with an indulgent shriek. The institutionalized empathy of a pet.

As sweat pooled beneath him on the loveseat, Redd looked past the sunburnt interns and, wavering in the distant heat, he saw someone leaning against a tractor, touching the brim of his hat, cigar sticking out the side of his face. It looked a lot like Lucious McVay.

July

"WHO IS that?" Redd asked the farmer's wife.

"That's the neighbor. He's a mechanic. Fixes all our very fine... machinery," she said.

"You sound bitter."

"My husband likes him, met him back when they were both doing some contract work on a Buddhist temple. I don't know. I just don't like all this talk about magic."

"His name McVay?" Redd asked.

"Yes. You know him?"

"He came into my bar once. Can't forget a guy like that I guess."

McVay indeed knew magic, babbled about its practitioners every chance he got. He railed against armchair alchemists, tome jockeys who never partook. Redd made himself listen, remembering those No Fear eyeball stickers they used to sell at Kroger beside the gumball machines and how his father wouldn't vend him one for a quarter to crank inside the slot. "Never display your weaknesses," his old man was fond of saying. Numerically, Redd was him now: an adult deprogrammed from childhood, free to turn his body into a laboratory everyone dumped their chemicals in.

"When do you stop waking up sore?" Redd inquired of his coworker Daryl, who, hoisting a forty-pound bag of fertilizer over one shoulder and completing bicep curls with an even heavier bucket of chicken scat, denied soreness altogether. As always, Redd regretted trying to connect.

An old red truck distributed their team of interns across the vast acres. Mary drove and, trying to avoid some low-hanging branches, slowly collided with the side of the house. She backed up, widened the crack, and stayed stuck, revving. McVay rounded the corner and ordered everybody out. When Mary didn't move, McVay said, "Will someone else grab the wheel please?" They heaved the truck bed apart from the house. Daryl feathered the gas. Mary hid behind a stinking mop of hair. McVay sang, "There is a crack, a crack in everything, that's how the light gets in," just to fuck with her.

Redd wormed through blackberry brambles. The sun was coaxed present when they took their sweaty shirts off. An expanding version of the human form chanted, sexlessly, for more spirits to light up. The dead held no real residence in the ground.

Group meetings went down on Thursday. Half the people here called the place an intentional community while the other half rolled their eyes at the phrase. Regardless, they all got to air grievances once a week. Human drama was the only entertainment. Petty arguments hastened the day. Redd conquered his fear of public speaking by speaking at every meeting even if he had nothing to say. Thursday was also his and Mary's day to cook the whole farm lunch, which gave him an hour alone with her every week. They roasted potatoes and carrots, stirred polenta, baked squash, and cooked a quinoa salad with raisins, nuts, and spices. Reaching under her shirt, he promised to quit cigarettes. She had a lot of vertebrae. He counted upward. She was secretly dating everyone.

"I'll let you cut my hair after work, if you want," Redd suggested.

"Already made plans with Daryl. Maybe this weekend," Mary said, beginning to weep.

Redd had studied palmistry and pathworking. People were shapeshifting into lesser Egyptian gods. His thoughts became hypermobile, that muscle in his head burning wider than the confines of his skull. The quotidian landscape dictated his form, and he frequently imagined himself as the texture of an oak tree, arms like dried morel mushrooms. Upside down in the roots of a more metaphysical earth, he could reproduce birds by the orgasm. He reiterated this vision to his coworkers at one of their Thursday meetings.

"Seems self-centered, or something," an intern interrupted.

"Solipthistic," another said, biting an apple.

"Don't talk with your mouth full!" the farmer's wife said.

"Redd, please continue," the farmer followed, stalling the return to work.

"Trees move and it only appears as if we were," Redd said.

"We haven't opened the omissions box," an intern said.

        "You mean the box of complaints?" someone else laughed.

        "You know we don't call it that," the farmer's wife said. "Plus, no one uses it, except for the Michelangelo who keeps drawing Dingo." The farmer's wife dumped the box that said *Sharing Is Caring* on its side. Sure enough, there was a drawing of the farmer's nearly dead dog named Dingo. She had an enormous head wound. Interns called it "The Oracle." Our world was Dingo's dream, the group concluded. The universe was a pus bubble afflicting an area just over Dingo's eye. Her cataracts and deafness had contributed to her being hit by the truck multiple times. Interns parasitically clinging to the vehicle would identify which giant bump was Dingo.

        A tattered title stood out on the bookcase above the farmer: *All Body, No Head*. Redd decided that the title had far outlived its ideas. Proliferating technology had substantially decreased our mastery from the neck down. The human brain was a feedback loop that led back to the Big Bang, an electromagnetic echo toppling everyone's lollipop headspace, a spiraling maze that could only be completed in sections. The relief of cutting off your arms and legs in dreams made every morning, in which they had regrown, its own punishment. Now Mary was off to the fields, balancing atop her two beautifully bony legs, with McVay. Or Lucious, as she purred. When Redd watched them walk away together, he pictured what the two of them would do all winter long, how easily the man could manipulate her frame, after all the interns had gone home. He pictured this, against his better judgment, and thought twice about his idea that humans had lost touch with their bodies.

When Redd asked her later what she and McVay would do all winter, she said, "In winter you gotta flush all the toilets once a day or the lines will freeze, takes up half the day right there." Then she told Redd that she and McVay would listen to podcasts together. She even made Redd a mixtape of people talking. One episode dealt with the average age of people in Japan. There were not enough caretakers for the elderly there. Redd sighed, no subtext to masturbate to, though when Redd closed his eyes he did see the constellation of moles, ribs, and spinal columns on Mary's back and he could smell her on the raised, rough surface of the compact disk. Concentrating, he could smell something deeper than skin. When you fist someone correctly, approaching the top of the colon, your hand might nick the heart. He smelled his finger, thinking about how holes are the heart's gateway drugs.

"It's been over an hour, Redd, what the hell are you doing?" the farmer's wife said.

Redd, startled from his daydream, got scolded for taking too long to finish the dishes, even though Mary had left him without a partner. They put him in the chicken coop for a night. Dingo was supposedly kept out there to scare away whatever had been taking bites of the cabbage. Occasionally, she forced some woofing. On the floor, in pain, Redd prodded the painful protrusion in his abdomen. Dingo's legs ran much more gracefully than they could when she was awake.

The next Thursday, Daryl raided the kitchen, diving toward a magnetic knife-strip on the wall, watching Redd and Mary. Mary's shirt resembled the kind of painting that wouldn't change much if she were stabbed.

"You two..." Daryl mumbled, running a blade against his thumbnail, as if testing an ice skate, "...interested in getting Chinese food?"

"What's the knife for?" Redd called after him.

"McVay needs help with a bull."

Redd pushed around the tempeh with a wooden spoon. Mary exhaled, almost disappointed that they hadn't been caught.

Alone in his hovel, Redd named everyone by their footsteps. The night air was being unbearably fucked by insects.

There was nothing but oats for breakfast. The bloating was a new excruciation.

"Power's out," Redd told the farmer. "My medication needs to be refrigerated."

"Let's see if McVay's got power." The farmer stared into his oatmeal, a glimpse of things to come. Women in the kitchen were high-fiving because their menstrual cycles had finally synched.

Two minutes on the farm bicycle or seven on foot got Redd from one farm to the other, a lot of wilderness between. There were so many animals that Redd couldn't add them all up in his head. He arrived with a box of refrigerated needles. As the sky went from black to pink, McVay met him in the foyer.

"They said you could stay and help me today," McVay said. He tucked a bandana into a cowboy hat to cover the back of his neck. "Follow me." Domestic beasts came first: dogs and cats. They both wore headlamps because the barn was still dark. In the barn, feed was thrown at horses, ducks, pigeons, chickens, and chicks. McVay showed Redd how to dunk a bucket into the feedbag. How many handfuls for each pair of legs. The rail they spread the pigeons' seeds on looked like an asteroid belt. Shells scattered across like meteors frozen in silver space.

"I'll show you how to clean one," McVay said, elbowing a chicken, which squawked. "If you want. The whole shebang."

McVay's overalls looked so stiff that they'd stand all

by themself. Ground rose with his boots. The stench of fresh hay lost to shit seeped onward. McVay had a dog named Sable that could deliver eggs to the front door one by one in its mouth. Redd feared to think that things might go easily. Sleeping with Dingo and her flies couldn't compare. Sable, the egg dog, glowed in the dark. Even her drool smelled good. She woke Redd with kisses. Sleeping at McVay's, he missed Mary and saw Daryl's haircut sitting in the center of every spider's web.

Redd and Sable walked a half-mile loop through tall grass. Sandhill cranes stood knee deep in water as blood cooled in one leg, warmed in the other, asleep upright. Sable sat on command. Redd saw the skunk before she did. Once she did, no command stopped her. The stink chased Redd through the thicket. Together they scrambled for tomato sauce, Sable screaming. Stripped to his underwear, Redd lathered himself and the dog with the closest thing: pizza sauce pre-mixed with onion, garlic, and basil. Sable paused and peered through the bugs, directly into Redd's eyes, an upgrade to the kind of looks he was used to, despite the sting of alliums.

August

REDD SCOURED a pan and allowed the soap bubbles to climb and remain on his arms since the skunk smell had continued to linger for the better part of a week. Layers of filth kept forming everywhere. Taking breath and body odor into consideration, Redd wouldn't have been surprised if the interns were cooking their own shit. Some kind of gut alchemy for herbivores. Redd wished he could've stayed longer at McVay's—less drama. Every day seemed dictated by the punishment suffered the day before. Now the farmer was behind him, speaking at the same frequency as the sink. The man had an elocution no amount of drink, sunlight, or hunger could quite affect. His timeworn face crunched out a grin.

Redd was ordered to the root cellar. The hinges creaked open. They squashed themselves down a labyrinth of hallways below the house. Nothing made architectural sense. Upstairs, water still ran. He was following a pair of overalls traced away by darkness. At some point, they scaled a second set of stairs. They were in a tunnel between houses. Glass jars on a rickety shelf clinked together. In the dark, the glasses wavered like a wheatfield. That theater Redd worked at in Detroit also had tunnels. There was much to bootleg during the auto industry boom. Walking this shaft felt like time turned inside out, a temporal moonwalk. Redd puffed condensation against a jar. He could feel the farmer's steps ahead of him. Air spread a pressurized hum, subconscious trumpet notes. Jars shrank with them as they walked. Or Redd was growing. They shared one calcifying heartbeat.

"This fucking mask," Redd hissed, tearing a spider web from his face.

The room was encased in glass. It smelled like a mass grave on fire. A horse blanket had been balled into the ground. Tons of equipment rusted out. A woman atop a dead tractor motioned them closer.

"You're our favorite uninitiated scarecrow," she cooed. "Ever look a scarecrow in the eyes?"

People laid down around them in a pattern, pressed against machines. Small cuts on their bodies seemed purposefully arranged. Redd had never seen his heart and therefore questioned its existence. He tried listening to something inside himself that wasn't just another voice. Dust trickled from the glass-domed ceiling. Lips moving like worms on her face, the woman sang of her own nudity. A severed head rolled up to her feet, issuing grotesque kissing sounds. A well-dressed body stumbled after, snatching Redd by the hair. "Ah, here it is," the head intoned, and the body began tugging. Redd screamed.

Everyone laughed. The body bent over, holding its stomach, like a mime in hysterics.

"In this guided meditation, you will scoop out the center of your brain. Notice the floor becoming cold. Cracks waver between their slatted wood. You've regrown your five senses. Know a second birth, a second death. Sing the eternal war between light and mud."

Daryl left that weekend. Redd fooled around with Mary more freely. He manipulated her small frame in order to stall his early and impending orgasm, but they embarrassed each other and no one finished. Working together would continue as foreplay for a satisfaction that'd never come. She left wearing only a white lab coat, one of her strange beachy accouterments. She wasn't worth adding to his body count.

Dumping rotten vegetables to the cows, Redd became elated that he'd never have to smell this brand of dung again. He flirted with other reeking interns.

McVay attended their final dinner, sweating, out of breath. "Roadkill deer down on Old US 12. Body's still warm."

"It's August."

"Fresh enough! Who wants to dress it up with me?"

McVay drove Redd to some adjacent land where the organs could rot at a distance. The deer's corpse slid around the truck bed, hooves clattering.

"Forgot the rope," McVay said. "Gonna have to field dress him."

They dragged it to a clearing. "Cut here," McVay said, hands crusted from his last kill. Redd held the deer by its skin, yanking the blade. Fur crackled free. Tissue, caught and matted, was raked smooth again. It smelled okay. Redd saw his reflection blurred black in an organ.

"Too bad she wasn't pregnant. Could've had us some veal," McVay said, spitting.

They carted away the hind legs, colored like children's balloons.

"Can I have the antlers?" Redd asked, surprising himself.

"Take 'em."

Redd snatched an ax from the back, squared a boot on the lolling head, and connected with the antler at its base. He had to keep chopping. There was nowhere to put the rack, so he carried it around, all jagged and blood slick.

The next time he saw Mary, he demanded: "Been riding any destroyed tractors?"

"You've been spending too much time with McVay," she droned.

"The never-ending intestine of occultism," he shuddered, testing his rage. "There is no real map for the human body." An Ezra Pound poem came to mind as he choked her.

September

REDD GENOCIDED whole colonies. Nothing from this land was innocent. He'd mercy shoot each coworker, even though their legs were intact. By some lopsided law they galloped free. The spool of the world ticked empty against these burnt-up volunteers. Mary should be done the slowest. He practiced on hornworms. Engorged pests, they nibbled away their camo. No teasing stimulation, no moral griping, just food. It was all dirt turning their insides neon. Redd gripped a horn on one of their rears and whipped the fat body to parts. Squelching goo still squirmed after he rubbed it in the soil. The harvest knife stayed glowing on his hip. Anything to lack humanity.

The interns took on other shapes at night.

Redd followed shadowed, hunched figures into the forest. He watched as they lit a fire and saw them as targets on the other end of it. They were ushering spirits from this pyre to lunar orbit. School-shooting casualties saluted Redd inside its smoke. He'd shut down every face in the hive of the flame. One woman, who Redd couldn't place, rambled about heavenly spheres blessèd and eternal as if they were ordered for the sake of the perishable world below.

"Know why they're called Bloomsburies," she asked, pointing at Virginia, the same head from his coma dream in January, who sat before him, grinning. Instead of floating in space it was being cradled by a headless, flat-chested woman. The talkative nude woman didn't wait for a response. "Because they only bloom when buried."

"Ghosts," she continued, "titter at our littleness, just as we smirk upon waking at the trifles and absurdities that loomed so large in dreams. Ghosts are minutia-free." A man who held his head as if on a platter, cut off at the neck, angled the face toward Redd. A Nordic visage bled through refraction, glaring at him grandpa-wise over his glasses.

"Smoke follows beauty," the head guffawed, squinting. The nude woman introduced a rain shower by sleight of hand. The fire went out and the figures scattered.

The following day, the farmer ran over Redd's foot with the tractor, crushing three superfluous bones. It was supposedly an accident. The physical therapy to follow temporarily distracted Redd's depression.

"I thought canning was for girls," whined another higher-up, Paul, swiveling in a piss dance toward Redd. "I wanna learn how to can." Paul's shorts were short enough to see last year's tan line. Redd often found Paul, in the middle of his shift, lying in the trough of potato mounds. Redd, not a snitch, napped with a stirrup hoe between rows of mustard greens. When he woke, he'd compare his pills to the passing clouds. Drinking made him talk and no one wanted that.

"I haven't had sex in six months," Paul said. "The thought is totally repulsive. But soon I might go nuclear on Grindr."

"Ever read 'The Rectum Is a Grave'?" Redd said. The entire swarm of interns approached Redd at his canning station, whispering about why he wasn't working standing up.

"Sounds delish!" Paul's mouth destroyed the words.

"Want to know the biggest secret about sex?" Redd spat. "Most people don't like it, but still feel the need to have it."

"I like sex," Suzie giggled.

"Slut," an intern chortled.

Mary chewed her hair. Suzie blushed. Daryl simply walked away. They were uncomfortable, pleasingly so. Redd wanted to watch them all walk across acacia thorns.

"How often do you think people here fuck?" Redd said, his thousand-yard stare holding them all in his peripherals.

The Ken doll guy frowned. "Less than ever this year."

Suzie lied to Redd about a cigarette she thought she caught him smoking. The creation of the erotic through the use of inorganics amazed her. "Lollipop sensation," she kept purring, her own idiot notion. "...the human skeleton without limbs, brain and stem floating in a vat, arms and legs grown back for punishment, a second head fused to the groin serving cold fellatio. Limbless wonder sucked to death by frostbite." She tugged the blouse off her nipples when she spoke. Palmistry was an excuse to seduce. A genuine rubbernecker of how people moved their bodies. Redd wanted to remember anything else.

Like many, Redd was disenchanted with his undergraduate studies. They had been reduced to teaching an organized emotion. He wasn't of an age then to think. The only worthwhile moment, outside a migraine, was when some Paul Valéry notebook fell into the aisle before him, directly at a passage describing how Edgar Allan Poe was the only writer who made a flawless synthesis of all the vertigoes. Redd shat himself reading it, possibly on purpose. He had already begun to carry spare underwear in his pack. Valéry's writing evoked images of a lucid dream, or an ocean, as if there was something real lurking beneath, something worth traveling deeper for. Words turned across the page like worms. Surrounded by glowing white tile, the soiled pair of boxer-briefs had stared back at him from the bottom of the can.

Redd was leaving the farm for good—his summer gig was up—but still somehow had Mary and Daryl in tow. They said that they were finally going to get that Chinese food. The three of them stopped at the credit union so Redd could deposit a couple hundred, the only money the farmers gave him for his four-month stint. A pair of attractive women in yellow robes approached him at the ATM, offering a free meal and laced sweets. They pointed across the street. Mary shrugged and Daryl leaned his head out the window and said, "Close enough." They followed the women across the street and through the orange and yellow threshold. The Hare Krishna bungalow hurt their eyes. The smell of incense was familiar to Redd, reminded him of the stench inside the barn.

"Why do we give in to our ego?" the lecturer posited during Bhagavad Gita class. Dogma was the price of the free meal. "Because we have, however momentarily, forgotten Krishna."

"Heinrich Himmler never forgot Krishna," Redd whispered to Mary. "He carried a pocket-sized Bhagavad Gita everywhere in his leather satchel. Sadly, I gave my copy away."

"To whom?" Mary cooed. She pronounced it like "tomb." When Daryl stood to piss, Redd squeezed her like he'd put her in one.

After dinner, they headed to the river, which was too wide to jump across and infinitely deep. Cement lined both sides. They ducked under a chain link fence. Mary scratched a hole in her elbow and couldn't swim.

"This is where I caught cholera jumping in," Redd said.

"We don't know that for sure," Mary said. "Walking barefooted on Belle Isle is a bad idea. The trip back is always worse than expected. The chain link snatches at your flesh. Partygoers' bottles fuck up the path. Branches lash you in the dark. So much mushroom cloud dawn."

"The Center for Disease Control and Prevention asked a lot of stupid questions on the phone."

"Heaven said you're a devil worshiper now," Mary said, apparently still in contact with her. "I think she just likes to say that, though."

"That's not really what we do. Mostly shock value. Performance art," Redd said, also untrue.

Heaven was just another ex the second they met. He should have known better as soon as random flakey words like LEVITATION and CRYSTAL trickled into his inbox. He preferred women when they twirled. In the only dream Redd had of Heaven, she exposed her breasts to strangers to upset him. "These do not belong to you!" she screamed. Something had attached itself to Redd that couldn't be scrubbed off.

"McVay seems serious," Mary said.

"All you guys are more self-help than Satanism," Daryl said. "More care than cult. Weirdest thing about self-help books is that someone actually had to write them." Redd fumed and refused to put his mental fire out with a good time. They wouldn't stop until they colonized the Milky Way. Redd had spent his last night on the farm initiating himself into McVay's strange cult. Laying on his back atop a small hill, Redd kept his eyes wide open and didn't move or sleep from sunset to sunrise. Fortified by the insane power of this memory, Redd smiled and watched Daryl hop into the river, another human sacrifice.

October

Even in youth, Redd enjoyed trauma, inflicted and endured. What he imparted was raked through his own fear with orgasmic intensity. The more he explored, the less stood in his way. The first time he posed naked in front of a group of female painters, robe casually folded and placed out of sightline, certain nightmares were realized.

A dive just west of Detroit, in a small township called Redford, sat in the pie slice of a five-way intersection, no walkable sidewalks in sight. The siding needed a power wash so badly that the lawn wasn't discernable from the building's crumbling exterior. Green gunk climbed between slats. He could smell his friends from the lot: candle wax, frankincense, animal blood.

The front door swung open, smashing the wall behind it. No one spoke. A game of pool halted. Redd tallied stares. A waitress drunkenly sang the rest of a song as the jukebox died. Eyes jittered like fireflies. He nodded to no one. A cook, squeezing blood from a patty, glared behind a stove that resembled a torture device. Some nerd balanced on a barstool asked for the entrance fee.

"I'm on the list," Redd said.

"Name?"

"I'm with McVay."

The kid licked a finger and flipped through his handout and adjusted his spectacles. Redd could see the note: *McVay + 4*. Green plastic dangles, hung throughout the establishment, cheapened an already polluted atmosphere. Lucious McVay and his posse arrived early, hoping to acquaint themselves with the veterans who had served in wars public school curriculums no longer required. A man introduced himself as Blind Willy, lifting his eyepatch to prove he'd just been released from the emergency room. Redd gave him enough for a drink, so he'd lower the flap.

What the cult was given for a green room wasn't as plush as Redd was accustomed to, especially since their Facebook group had taken off, stretching past forty thousand. Their followers mostly thought it was a meme page, not a Theistic Satanist account. The best kind of magic was unintentional, subliminal, and cheeky. Satanic grandad Anton LaVey claimed curses worked best on those vehemently denying their possibility. Redd enjoyed the crunch of a djinn sinking its teeth into these fools, the cursed body shriveling inside a cacodemonic mouth, the arms of modern medicine flopping helplessly above, like a woman performing reiki. Not even Catholics, silently giving birth to Satanism, consecrating profit, could locate its coordinates. Surrounded from the inside, there was no escape.

Something beneath the table's torn felt was too wet to be wood. The barred windows provided no view. Patrons seated at the bar swiveled so they didn't have to look at Redd. He stank beneath his leather jacket. The green tea he'd packed in his satchel had gone cold. He continued steeping even though he hated the astringent flavor. Yet another habit he hadn't kicked since living with his ex. The air around his fridge still stank of her perfume. When food spoiled, mixing with the stench, it smelled like his fingers did after spending an afternoon inside her. The girl's habits had always bothered him, but when he voiced this she sang her famous refrain: "You'll miss me when I'm gone." He assumed she meant for the day, but she had meant forever. Either way, she was mistaken.

Redd approached the bar where Lucious McVay, the hierophant of Redd's coven, was seated, surrounded by groupies. This lowkey watering hole was the perfect place for their event. Lucious knew the booking agent, otherwise this kind of show wouldn't fly. Redd nervously played with the keys in his pocket and thought about his Nissan. The "Direction" function on the touchscreen took him wherever he needed to go, told him when and where to turn, and adjusted the seat to his proportions. There were two presets on the left side of the driver's seat, but he'd only ever set the first, as no one else had driven the car, and this depressed him. Weakened by emotion, his cervical spine drooped. He closed his eyes, counting deep breaths, a process detailed in the pseudonymous sex magic book he'd been picking through. The author claimed he didn't want to use his real name because the techniques were illegal. More likely, Redd thought, it was out of embarrassment for authoring a self-help book. He had no desire to know anybody who wrote that flavor of garbage and hated himself for reading it. But Redd knew what he wanted. The hidden knowledge of techniques described by such sociopaths presented bountiful opportunities for pussy.

McVay sparked philosophical questions in Redd. His long, Sadhu-like beard attracted bar-goers, ditto his leather jacket studded with Sabbath and Bathory patches, Azathoth and Asmoday pins. McVay had a gravitational pull Redd was not immune to. Upon Redd's approach, he tugged his beard and cleared his throat. They watched their shadows cross. Lights flickered, dulled by dust. The woman tending bar pressed her chest to the counter. The lines on her cleavage seemed burnt there.

"Black Label, please," Redd said.

"Comin' up," she said, stumbling backward. Before she disappeared behind the curtain, she caught Redd's eye and shook a pint of Captain Morgan above her ass like mistletoe. He figured she would pour some in his beer, but Redd never saw her again.

It was October thirtieth—Devil's Night. The sun struggled to warm the other side of the world. Valleys and lakes didn't take heat without asking to unload something of their own. Everything was a quid pro quo. The whole of humanity craved exchange. It'd be better if the globe swallowed itself in flame.

Jennifer Aniston's face glitched across the television above the bar. The captions running beneath her chin were slightly delayed, but it seemed as if she'd devolved into an experimental performance artist who still had enough money to advertise her happenings. She described her newest piece called "Time to Go," in which she recorded herself urinating as much as possible in a twenty-four-hour period, drinking only water and diuretics. Redd looked around, but everyone, including people behind the bar, were glued to their smartphones, processing other, more personal data. Posture can tell you a lot about a person's discipline.

Redd hated the way the bad habits of his generation, with their hunched personalities, slouched across the globe, a virus that he tried to double over in himself. Fight sickness with sickness. Even though his initial attraction to the occult stemmed from finding common ground with his ex, the breathing exercises, pathworking, and meditation did make him feel more like himself, even if that self was outrageously violent and subservient to uncontrollable urges to harm himself and others. There was a freedom in trying to put theory into practice, at least until he tried talking about it, which made him feel like a caged child and like anything except the thing itself. There was nothing false about that religious, oceanic feeling he got when taking a long walk at night, or standing at the edge of a scenic cliff, although the buzzing union he felt with the world around him was mysteriously difficult to describe. As if in response to his inner thoughts, when he looked back at the television, Aniston's face was replaced by yet another advertisement.

"What's your shirt say?" Redd elbowed McVay's black jacket.

"If you want to have a miserable afternoon, listen to these guys. 'Buyer's Market.' What does that mean to you?"

Redd didn't answer because he was studying the way that the wrinkled girl's face on the shirt looked surprisingly like Aniston's. They had the same eyes.

"Cheap. Life is cheap." McVay produced a bulimic laugh. "Cool with being the flesh altar tonight?"

"Sure," Redd said. "You have a robe?"

"Should be in the box with the Asmoday flag."

Redd nodded, resting his feet on a metal step, toeing the cheap architecture. Brown and white bottles were lit red. Light stuck inside the necks like spit. Fresh air closed itself off from attendees, but remained a prospect for those who'd stay until they reached the other side. Electricity whizzed beneath them, humming tunes only little girls know, one of Satan's many lairs, an underaged throat. Paint eclipsing the beauty of every Redford woman in this establishment had dried with a lack of fluidity, crumbling bits of visage. Redd scraped his shoe through a pile. Chatting here and there with people he'd met online, who tried to appear interesting (they never were through his end of the screen), he wondered why the big guy downstairs required so much guyliner. Perhaps tear-like black streaks down the faces of men could break through the perennial mask. Truth was something too terrifying to appear on the surface, needing to be coaxed out of the ever-expanding dark.

"Redd and I work together at the bookstore," McVay lied, interrupting Redd's daydream.

"We get to see entire libraries come in, and skim the cream off the top," Redd laughed.

"You speak so lightly of knowledge," the woman sitting next to them said. She wore cat eye makeup. "Is the mingling of lightness with Satanism ever followed by buying a lady a drink?"

McVay held up a finger to the nonexistent bartend. His arm swooped around his victim and moved her toward the restroom. As they vanished into the meth haze developing behind the door, Redd's eye caught the light outside. He briefly mistook a glowing burger sign for the moon. Redd exercised asceticism, refraining from a compulsory cigarette, but when McVay left with the girl, he felt trapped. Floating adjacent to a nothingness in which he didn't belong, he decided to go for a smoke. As the cult set the stage for the ritual, a GIF of him blinking through his smoke replayed in his mind. In the lens of the CCTV, he glimpsed the intricacies of a world clouding fuller, blurring faster than this one, the way you could sometimes, mysteriously, witness the blood vessels of your own eye when a physician closely inspected God's work through an ophthalmoscope.

There were four people in the audience, all on their phones, but it was hard for Redd to see out of his *Eyes Wide Shut*-style mask. The clock was about to strike midnight, beginning a new Halloween. Most patrons moved to an adjacent room to continue drinking. They played pool and balanced large leprechaun hats on their noses, not understanding why McVay and Redd didn't play music. McVay rang his dinner bell three times. The ritual commenced. Their cult echoed the names of every devil in Anton LaVey's *Satanic Bible*, much to the annoyance of the waitstaff.

"Belial!" they shouted.

"Lilith!"

"Jupiter!"

Redd recalled a passage from *The Lesser Key of Solomon*: "The spirits of the Goetia are portions of the human brain. Their seals therefore represent methods of stimulating or regulating those particular spots." He didn't know if King Solomon thought this himself, or if it was the interpretation of those carrying on his tradition, but it was easier if ceremonial magic appealed to the logic of the culture. Pop science took center stage, which meant, at first anyway, demons were not somewhere Out There, floating around in space, but In Here, as close to home as ever. He felt lighter than a speck of dust, a mote in the eye of the earth.

One of the newer initiates wobbled. Her four-inch platforms didn't get along with all the Vodka Red Bulls. Her eyes rolled back. She yelped, failing to stabilize against an amplifier, knocking over a chalice of pig's blood. The cup clattered to the floor. Purple blood followed a trail of guitar cables, disappearing beneath an amp.

"Fuck," someone said.

"We needed that blood to cleanse the flesh altar," another one said.

Redd's anxiety about the spill dissolved into relief. He hadn't gotten the memo about a goblet of blood being dumped on him. Who knew what bacteria coagulated within. "Perhaps you could summon a demon to clean up," Redd quipped. His insides felt gnawed on by creatures gaining sentience as they diminished him.

Language, call and response, and the music of the event lodged within the cult and affected them deeper and stronger than anything done in solitude. Even King Solomon, who supposedly chased seventy-two spirits into a deep hole in Babylon, binding them because of their pride, documented the event to share with his friends. In his testament, he tells the story of how he took dozens of wives, all worshiping strange gods, and aided them in their devotion. He once crushed grasshoppers into a fine powder and offered it to Moloch to sleep with Eros herself. It made Solomon weak and he spent the rest of his days building temples to false idols until his bones wilted.

"Don't worry, I'll mop it," Burton, the Adeptus, said. Although Adeptus used to designate caretakers of certain occult knowledge, in this context it referred to a rung on the nonexistent ladder of hierarchy in the cult.

"Zealator, come forth!" That's what they called Redd, mainly because he looked like a Jew. Lucious McVay held his hands before him, palms upward. Redd shuffled toward the giant red X on the floor where the drum set would have been if they were a band.

"Do you consent to be our altar of flesh for this evening; to serve Satan and all his whims; to inspire a connection to the other world?"

"I do!" Redd said.

"Take off your clothes!"

Redd tore the robe from his body and knocked against one of McVay's candles, which teetered. Redd knelt, hands high above his head. Nude, the power dynamic between him and the crowd shifted in his favor. Americans couldn't resist elongating their lenses. Redd was no exhibitionist, but he loved the feeling of turning an audience into peeping toms. Through two small holes in the mask, he saw Burton unclasp a hunting knife from his hip, face the crowd, and scream. Burton pretended to carve two deep incisions in his forearm, hunching over in agony for effect. Redd continued to assume this was an act, since when Burton turned around and approached him, the arm looked like a pristine slab of marble, but then an enormous cross opened candy apple red, erupting faster than he had ever witnessed. This impression only lasted a moment before Burton overfilled the chalice with drippings and dumped it over Redd's head. Everyone screamed. McVay laughed and yelled "Hail Satan!" No one heard him. Burton couldn't stop the blood. Redd began his glossolalia, swaying beneath the spout. Burton's adrenaline spiked. He rubbed his arm all over Redd. Redd was deep in his role and forgot about his fear of foreign bacteria. He reveled in it, painted from head to toe by warmth. The small audience of four took a couple steps back. Blood fell silently to the floor among the screams of the stragglers and absorbed into Redd's clothes, which he'd tucked beneath the table, thinking they'd be safe there.

Pool balls cracked in the adjacent room. The players' mouths hung open, as if inviting whatever the space was slowly filling up with. They wanted nothing to do with the liberal costume party going on in the other room. The teetering candle finally fell on the Asmoday flag, catching fire. McVay began desecrating a Bible, tearing and balling up its pages, engulfing them in flames, tossing them into the nearly empty audience like a game of hot potato. One of them accepted an invitation to stomp on a wooden cross, breaking it with a heel kick. McVay held out the Good Book and yelled, "Eat it!" A woman shoved a page between her teeth and fell to her knees in mock revelation.

The bartender was passed out in the back room, covered by a horse blanket, beside an empty bottle of rum. Redd never got the beer he ordered. As the blood trickled into his eyes and nose and mouth, it wasn't that he forgot about his thirst, but it no longer seemed to matter, like holding urine until you no longer had to go.

In the restroom, Redd cleaned the blood from his face. He felt stoned but hadn't done any drugs. He wondered if this is what his grandmother meant, if he could trick himself into pleasure without supplicating those who tended bars or sold drugs from the backseats of their lemons. Cold water remained on his face as he left the establishment. The others would clean up the fire and mess. He'd done them a favor by being the flesh altar beneath an open arm. Germs whose footprints remain are called bloodborne pathogens. Redd felt a twinge in the back of his throat, wiping fluid too thick to be water from his eye. Symptoms of certain demons might be extraordinarily mild, might start six months after contact. Sometimes there were no symptoms. He heard a squawk and looked up at something large and buoyant moving quickly through the branches of a tree. It was just the moon.

November

REDD'S FACE inflated across the doorknob. Locked in a toilet, taking razors to either naked leg, he smeared his costume shinier, cut slant holes in meat, the leash of an artery. His ex had a cheese pizza demeanor. She was soon to be released. He'd off himself again and again in her honor, or take her place at the asylum. That bitch loved blood. For legal reasons, they texted Redd her whereabouts. He spat in his self-inflicted wound and counted the bubbles. It was a rather erotic balancing of humors. An eyeball slit by hair, hers, seemed to wink from the drain.

His ex's eyes were green. No one could treat her. She was too busy catwalking in a straightjacket, body wiry with ballet and caffeine. She referred to Redd as "Angel" without irony. Free an hour, she texted Redd to visit. Approaching, after a year apart, they froze at the same time, drunk with each other. He squeezed her swaying ass on the walk up her mother's stairs. They fucked in silent intervals all night. Hoisting her onto the bathroom countertop, with marijuana smoke pouring from his nostrils, he liked her robe half undone, raw dogging those innards until she renounced God. He drank sweat from her bellybutton. She made him breakfast—shaved ginger root over hand-picked berries, vanilla ice cream, and melted chocolate—even initiated a blowjob while her mother stomped around just outside the door. Redd considered asking if she'd join them.

Redd put up with the shit the ex said to keep warm during the winter. She got drunk and made him fight people, meanwhile thumbing her phone. He was duped enough to text her about his dreams. His latest consisted of a rocking horse constructed of his bones. The boys in the ward had had trouble getting hard, she whined.

They walked deep into the woods without looking. "Come in with me," Redd said. The Krishna building entrance opened before them. This brand of Hinduism revived a transcendental group consciousness through an eight-syllable-per-line quatrain installed in the foreground of many minor Upanishads. The words wiped away the mess the world had made of their faces. She paused, hypoglycemic blood ricocheting through her body. Indian babies scooted across the floor. Insect eggs hatched in their diapers. The ex became a manifestation of Krishna's purple skin as the theremin lured her.

"Are orbs souls?" one devotee asked.

"How does the verse say to measure?" the teacher said.

"A hundredth of the tip of a hair," another replied.

Redd meant to strip the reality from this figure, strove to blast metaphor into existence person by person.

He wanted his ex to squirt in a telephoto lens, fuck the glass back into herself, squirm down to a skeleton. She was another carbon-copy addict fit for the operating table.

She talked him into attending the Fillmore. For most of its history the building had been known as the State Theatre, but the theater—like the names of notorious neighborhoods—had been rebranded to drive sales. Near downtown Detroit, the Fillmore sat across Woodward from Comerica Park, formerly Tiger Stadium, where Redd attended ball games as a kid. Every blank façade had fruitlessly gentrified.

Radiohead had shot to popularity the day Redd was born with a slacker anthem underscoring his existence. Their songs were catchy until you looked at what you caught. Millennials were so concerned with sharing their stories, and pictures of their lunch, that they had deepthroated their own microphones, which may have been the origin of such needless feedback, feedback that Redd wished Radiohead's fans would have embraced fully, actualizing the band's "I don't belong here" lyric.

His ex was the prettiest groupie in the pile. Redd bit her when they kissed. The crowd parted around them. Redd's skin felt screwed on. A dim river of bodies slipped through itself, puddles of beer and squeezed limes. He had smuggled drugs past security before and accomplished much worse today. Once, at an electronic music show, two wasted sluts pressed their tits against him to use his gigantic hair as a security blanket and a couple of spliffs fell out. Knowing how to navigate the dark web, a patchwork of soft links between suburban basements where odd poisons and strange military technologies were made available, brought Redd comfort, even a certain peace. Employing bitcoin, avoiding bots, copying the transaction ID, awaiting confirmation, his tools were sizable.

The ceiling looked like a starving mandala. A sexless, blob-shaped security guard posed less a threat than the music. His ex was halfway through frottage with herself. She pressed her thin snout in a baggie of coke, then broke her own necklace trying to make Redd finger her. He offered to crawl after the pieces, but she'd already taken it as a sign, crying. A number of dudes approached, openly trying to console her in front of him. "Hey baby. This guy bothering you?" Redd checked his hardware. People were still bobbling in. He left her to her men, squirting liquid LSD into a series of drinks as he passed. By the time she was swallowing some stranger's come, the crowd was congesting near the stage. Redd was prepping canisters of tear gas.

He rallied himself in a restroom. Double-tapped the screen of his phone. Heaven had gone mute when she had left him for her ex-boyfriend, the chef, prior to Redd's stint on the farm. Yet here she was, after all these months, in his inbox. "I've been thinking about this a long time," Heaven's text began, "and I've had many conversations with friends." The bitch had written Redd a novel. He scrunched his eyebrows together and continued. Like everyone her age, she wrote like a dilettante addressing her fan club. "First I had to accept myself as a victim of your biting. But I am proud to say that I now identify as a survivor." Redd recalled when she had cut him, sexily, during BDSM play. Her new victim arc was the crestfallen identity our cultural narrative had handed her, which is what he was here to address. He sent her a picture of his erection shooting its final rope of come into the busted toilet, then dropped the phone into it with a splash.

Someone had scribbled GENDER RESUSCITATION in big black letters over the restroom door. He zip-tied the only entryway into the theater, shooting the first security guard to approach. As the screaming mass wobbled forward, he singled out target upon target. They looked like the bullets were making them orgasm, climbing toward a death he fucked them into. He disappeared inside their panic, snatching from the tangle of arms and legs, arteries popping like chicken necks. People were sliding great distances into themselves. There was no difference between the lyrics and the audience's cries for help. Covering the stage, the fire seemed pyrotechnic, at which a select few continued to cheer. A throb of light twitched out at the same death rattle as the rest. Everyone was just a set of quieted veins. He saw his ex, stripped down to her white bra on the floor, getting bled on by some still-hard amputee. She was smiling as Redd finished her, looking somehow directly into his eyes, a frozen look from what seemed miles off. This was their best date by far.

In the smoke from her forehead, he saw the farm, Lucious McVay's giggling exhaust, the dogs he should have shot too, a slug in the universe's canine eye. He carried himself down the drain never with enough company. Redd snapped awake with three heads in space rolling toward him, gibbering.

Darkness was not something Redd fell toward, but through.

December

I SHIVER in the shadows of this vacant city where a cell tower has disassembled the light. My remains stink like secondhand clothes. I am stuck together with nails stolen from a coffin. The streets are full of dead relatives, airing out.

These very governmental creatures came donning tote bags. They sold hyper-speed connectivity, ultra-low latency. There was no gun left with which to question them. All there was was art supplies. We knew we would regret the build, but needed more shimmery cancers to color ourselves in with. Pixelated treasure chests exploded behind our eyes. Families scattered under the mast, cackling blood. I looked at the metals overhead like a woman soaping her back. It felt like you ate ice cream from the womb. Our speech melted in its socket. Bodies filled with indigestible materials. My guts would sculpt nothing into shit anymore, except the rest of me.

I began shaking maracas to communicate. An angry neighbor arrived to paint my portrait unflatteringly. His idiot son rubbed a microphone on his wrist, trying to broadcast the suicide. Words formed out the hole. Something discernible beyond rustling blood. My aunt, half her body laying an egg of itself, told everyone to shut up. Maybe the boy's ghost could articulate her deficiencies. I smashed my skull with podcasting equipment until everything I thought came stupidly loose. We said what we could while conscious. The boy's lips split, locked together in gore, as he said things elsewhere, bashing himself an alphabet.

Free of any memorial, through the digital snow I call a face, despite the byproducts beneath my waste, still I call out to the fallen.